Gay Z

Tales of Seeking
and Discovery

Mike McClelland

Beautiful Dreamer Press

Gay Zoo Day
Copyright 2017 by Michael McClelland

Beautiful Dreamer Press
309 Cross St.
Nevada City, CA 95959
U.S.A.
www.BeautifulDreamerPress.com
info@BeautifulDreamerPress.com

A version of "Sheffield Beach" first appeared in *Queen Mob's Teahouse*.
A version of "Gay Zoo Day" originally appeared in *ImageOutWrite* (Vol 5, September 2016).
"The Self-Banished" first appeared in *ink&coda,* Issue 3.1.
A version of "La Castaña" originally appeared as "Flyboys and Cowboys" in the anthology *Cowboy Roundup* (JMS Press, 2016).

Paperback Edition
Printed in the United States of America

ISBN: 978-0-9981262-2-7

Library of Congress Control Number: 2017932302

Cover design by Tom Schmidt
Front and back photography by Dot
Author photo by Casey McClelland

for Mom and Dad

CONTENTS

Gay Zoo Day

Tales of Seeking

and Discovery

✳ ⁊ ★

SHEFFIELD BEACH

✠

Two fat, dappled dachshunds greet me at the door of the beach house, baring their teeth and growling with such savagery I actually look behind myself to see if a stray dog or vervet had come through the security gate behind my rental car.

Isabelle, my hostess for the long New Year's weekend, sweeps past them, opening her arms, though we don't really know each other well enough to embrace. She talks as she walks towards me, arms outstretched, like she's approaching something heavy that needs to be picked up and put away somewhere.

"Max, you're so tan you look black! They're always antsy around blacks. You should see them with the poor maid. If she doesn't have her uniform on, they act like she's a burglar. And don't even *ask* about the gardeners."

I've been in South Africa long enough to no longer be shocked by such revelations.

I don't even like Isabelle. She's rich and stupid. She's a junior account executive on another of my agency's clients, and she had latched onto me as soon as I'd transferred into the office, eager for an American friend. Isabelle is desperate to move to New York someday, to live some version of *Sex and the City* and to "get away from all of South Africa's terrible crime."

I've not yet felt compelled to tell Isabelle that New York is more dangerous than Rivonia, the one percent enclave north of Johannesburg where she lives most of the year, and it's certainly more dangerous than our current location, Sheffield Beach, just north of Durban on KwaZulu Natal's Dolphin Coast. I learned quickly that it's pointless to argue with rich, white South Africans about crime. They, almost without exception, live in palatial homes behind high walls and sit in terror as they imagine the walls shrinking in on them, the black tide pulsing and boiling just beyond.

I look around the beach house, trying not to gape. Isabelle told me it was a cottage, her parents' third home. Her parents were in Switzerland, leaving Isabelle to host friends at the cottage for the long New Year's weekend. There is nothing cottage-like about this place, though. Beyond the snarling dachshunds lay a massive white-tiled living and dining room, decorated tastefully in creams and blues. Beyond that, the far wall is entirely glass, revealing a gorgeously appointed deck and an untainted view of the beach and the roaring Indian Ocean beyond. On both sides of the large living room, Escher-like staircases climb up and down to what must be bedrooms. Isabelle had informed me, upon invitation, that the "cottage" had four bedrooms, which to be fair had seemed like quite a bit of bedrooms for a cottage. There would be four couples staying in addition to Isabelle's single cousin Ruben and myself, who would be sleeping on ("comfy! and private!") couches.

"Margie! Taffy! Shut the fuck up!" Isabelle screeches, and the snarling little beasties skitter off across the tiled floor to hide under an overstuffed leather chaise.

"Rosie is just doing some laundry and then she can make you something for lunch. Or, you're free to help yourself to anything," Isabelle tells me as she looks me up and down. "Was your flight quite ghastly? You look terrible!" she laughs.

Bitch. I hold up a duty free bag. "Here, some booze," I say, hoping she'll offer to open it up even though it's only 11:30.

"Oh, you angel!" she squeals as she takes the bag. Her nasal accent makes 'angel' sound obscene.

Unburdened by decorum, Isabelle rips open the bag and appraises its contents. Two bottles of Patron—one silver, one coffee—and four bottles of Moët. She smiles approvingly and then says, "Shall we have a little tot on the veranda? Everyone else is napping. We had a bit of a jol last night!"

Eager to sit by the ocean and to drink myself to a better opinion of Isabelle, I nod.

"Where should I put my bag?"

"Oh just leave it here by the door. Rosie will take it up. You're sleeping in my dad's office. He has the coziest couch by the window. Rosie's got all the linen laid out for you already, so if you need to nap, just go ahead. Ruben is sleeping on the couch *just* around the corner from you, if you fancy some company."

I'm too tired and polite to roll my eyes, so I pretend to be distracted by a piece of art, a vaguely cubist oil painting of some ancient sea tale, complete with a sea monster and a dismembered sailor, rendered in (of course) cream and blue.

Isabelle heads around the corner to the right, to what I assume is the kitchen. Of course she wants to set me up with her cousin. In addition to aiding her in her mission to become my *bestie* (her word, not mine), any sexual exploit that I undertake will give her plenty of ammunition in the office gossip hierarchy. *Why the fuck am I here?*

Because I had to be back in time to start work on the second (unheard of in South Africa, but my boss is German) and I hadn't wanted to spend New Year's alone in my apartment in Newtown. That's exactly what I should have done, though. Ringing in the New Year with a junior staff member and her desperate cousin—and seven other surely horrible strangers—was idiotic. I'd been seduced by the mentions of pristine beaches where I could run and run for miles and an ocean warm enough to swim in. When making the arrangements I'd been willing to overlook the company, but in the here and now my prospects feel bleak.

I slip through the sliding glass doors and lean against the deck railing. The roar of the ocean encompasses me. The white beach below is flecked with people, probably only ten total in the half mile of beach visible before it disappears around a rocky cusp. The cottage juts out just far enough on a bluff that I can only see the neighboring houses if I crane my neck. The homes along the beach are all modern monstrosities; blocky, glassy monuments to money. This could be any beach in the world, except for the thin black line dividing the bluffs holding the homes with the beach below. That thin black line is a high iron fence crowned with razor wire. All beaches in South Africa are public. The folks at Sheffield Beach have gotten around that by concealing the public access paths between security fences and planting as many shrubs along both sides as possible, making access from the street level nearly impossible. Apparently a few Indian fishermen make their way through every day, but Isabelle assured me that "they aren't dangerous; just tacky."

A tap on my shoulder tells me Isabelle has joined me and I turn to see her standing with a tray holding three shot glasses, the bottle of silver tequila I'd brought, a lemon, and a small bowl of salt. Are these people too rich for shakers?

Behind Isabelle stands a tall, skinny, pale-skinned twenty-something in a polo shirt and incredibly short golf shorts, which reveal well-formed, if unmuscular, legs. His face is attractive in an aristocratic way: full, wet lips and upturned nose, the kind of face you want to either slap or fuck. *Jesus, listen to me.* I need a nap.

"Max, this is Ruben, my cousin. Ruben, this is the colleague I was telling you about. Max is running the Absa account brilliantly, and we're lucky to have him."

I marvel at how Isabelle is able to use my accomplishments to pad her own résumé. I'm about five levels above her in seniority and she has no idea how well I'm running the Absa account.

"It's a pleasure to meet you, Ruben."

I reach towards him for a handshake. Ruben is apparently not used to such gestures. He juts a hip out and kangaroos his arms up to his sides.

"Look at how polite he is, Bells. I thought Americans were *rough*," he says out of the side of mouth with a gross smirk. He says "rough" like it's a request and I'm instantly repulsed and aroused by him.

Isabelle giggles idiotically and pours three overflowing shots. We all lick our fists and liberally pour the salt in anticipation.

"To new *friends!*" Isabelle growls before licking the salt and downing the shot. Ruben sips his tequila with his pinky out, grimaces, and then downs it with a shiver. I gulp mine and hold up my glass for another.

"Keep them coming."

✠

After a shower and a quick nap, I return to the deck to find Isabelle and five others sitting in a hot tub that I hadn't noticed before. I almost trip over two empty Moët bottles lying beside the tub. *Assholes.* Isabelle looks tanked already, her hair stringy and eyes unfocused.

"We opened the champagne! Don't worry, I can take you to buy some more tomorrow."

She's splotchy, bright red patches interlacing across her neck and shoulders like splitting amoebas. It's probably ninety degrees out, and humid, so surely the hot tub is doing nothing to help her disposition. She is seated on the lap of a humongous ginger who has surely been bred for the killing of animals and the playing of rugby.

The giant holds up a hand. "Byron. You must be Max?"

Isabelle looked from Byron to me and then hisses at him, "Don't interrupt!" though no one seems to be talking.

I nod at Byron and introduce myself to the others, who are

all so generically white and expressionless that their names vanish from my mind upon entry. I consider asking them how my champagne tastes, but there's no use pissing them off right away. I'm sure I'll do it eventually without having to try.

"I'm going to go for a run," I tell Isabelle. "Can I just let myself out of the gate?"

"The keys are in the scullery," Isabelle slurs. "But careful ... it's hot! And there was a mugging on the beach last week."

Of course there was. Any time you state an intended destination to a South African, you hear, "It's lovely *but* a good friend of mine was mugged there." Or stabbed. Or shot.

Byron apparently hadn't heard this before. "You're kidding! On Sheffield Beach?"

Isabelle hiccups before continuing, her eyes sobering in the dramatic retelling. "Yes, three black gentlemen," (black crime-doers were often "gentlemen" in white South African stories, lest accusations of racial bias arise) cornered Mr. Van De Merwe from down the road and stole his shoes at knifepoint! It's so isolated down there, no one was around to help. Of course, it could have been *so much worse.*"

"Fucking *kaffirs*," Byron says under his breath.

That word. It's a very rude word, one that shouldn't be used. It's like the *N* word in America.

The other hot-tubbers pretend not to hear him, though I

imagine they secretly agree. Byron turns to me and says, "Be careful, friend. Though you're more likely to get hit by a rogue wave and washed out into the riptide. Stay close to the bluffs. High tide is at five so you'll either want to go right away or wait until after."

Certain I can't take Isabelle's company at the moment, I thank Byron for the advice and go to the scullery to find the keys.

✠

I get to the beach and set out at as swift a pace I can manage in the sand. I've not run on the beach in quite some time and it's always a challenge readjusting to the rigors of running through shifting sand. The hot sun beats down gloriously and I throw my tank top off, letting the sun rake over my skin. The beach is almost entirely abandoned.

I round the rocky cusp and am delighted to find an unobstructed portion of beach that stretches for what looks like miles. To my right, waves crash dramatically, roaring over the rocky beach and into the delicate white sand, reaching towards my sneakered feet. To my left, high bluffs rise severely out of the sand, their rocky surface covered in dense swaths of thorny bushes.

The bushes are incredibly dense. I wonder what could be watching me from within. Sea turtles? Pelicans? *Criminals?*

I continue along, marveling at the brilliant whiteness of sand. Quite suddenly, hundreds of crabs come into view. They've been here all along, their white bodies camouflaged. They are grotesque, all skittering left to right as they sense my presence, searching for wet sand where their little claws can find purchase and dig a hidey-hole. As they bury themselves, they look like little skulls sinking into quicksand.

I begin to sweat in earnest and the combination of the salty sweat and direct sunlight on my chest gives me a breathless, erotic feeling. Soon my short blue shorts are soaked nearly through with sweat, exposing the outline of my briefs, and I wonder if I could just strip and run naked through the sand. I can see no other souls in front or behind me, and the thought of running naked down a wild beach sends a surge through me, giving my legs second life.

I resist the urge to discard my shorts, but my mind begins to wander. What if I *were* mugged on the beach? What if I rounded this next bend and was met by two or three hungry black vagrants, eager to take my shoes? Should I have run barefoot?

Stop thinking like this. This is obscene. There are no black vagrants hiding in the bushes waiting to steal your shoes.

But *what if?* What if they are starving? There have been no fish to catch for days and then suddenly I emerge from around the bend, like a mirage, my sweaty naked skin shining in the sun. The full muscles of my meaty legs making them hungry, their starving minds unable to control their basest urges. What if they attack me? Could I run away? Surely I'm stronger, but I'm heavier. I would sink in the sand as I ran away while their light bodies flew over it, emboldened by hunger.

Five. Shirtless, lean, and hungry. Their eyes turned feral by starvation and subjugation. They'll corner me and I'll plead, fall to my knees. I'll give them my shoes but they'll throw them to the side. It's me they want. Their teeth raking my skin. Biting into me. Pulling me apart. The blood stains their white teeth and it's so dark that it matches the bruised, wounded color that the sun has burnt into their black cheeks. They savagely rip me to shreds, relishing every bite, and I know I let this happen to myself, that I let them pick me clean.

Stop it. This is sick.

My legs are burning; I've been running too hard.

What the fuck am I doing?

I glance at the bushes, suddenly fearful.

They wouldn't eat you, you idiot. They'd take your shoes. Maybe rape you.

But I'd fight them off. I'd grab a piece of driftwood—no, sea glass—and as they fell upon me I'd slash and scream. Adrenaline would flood my system and I'd crack one's neck before severing another's jugular with my glass weapon.

I'd return to the cottage, covered in blood, and everyone would rejoice in my survival. I'd call the police and make national, international news. At home, I'd grant one tasteful interview with—who is the Oprah of today?—probably still Oprah—where I would emphasize that it wasn't about race, it was about survival. About right and wrong, living and dying.

I round another cusp and reach a lagoon. The lagoon is quickly filling as a result of a small-but-growing stream curling across the beach from the ocean. The bluffs move dramatically inland around the lagoon, forming a series of small, shady inlets along the lagoon's far edge. I consider exploring them, getting out of the sun for a bit. But the tide is coming in, and if I cross the small stream now it might be too wide for me to cross upon my return.

Reluctantly, I turn around and run back. The crabs are all still in hiding, the bushes still silent.

✠

At dinner, we all drink more and play a few stupid games. Never-have-I-ever and the like. I'm the star, given my nationality and the fact I'm a couple of years older than everyone else. *Really, why the hell did I come here?*

At night, Ruben sneaks up while I'm lying on the tiny office couch and asks me if I'm cold as well. I've played this game before; he wants me to tell him to join me, that I'll make him warm.

Fucking him seems like far too much effort, finding a condom and lube and then dealing with the inevitable emotional fallout of having been inside such a fragile creature. Instead, I sit up and pat the couch next to me. He sits down nervously and begins to whisper something in the way of conversation. I shut him up by kissing him—his mouth is too soft and unpracticed, but eager. He goes down to suck me off and I don't stop him. While he's doing it, he moans and squeals and swishes his floppy dark hair around and I wonder what is happening to him down there. I ignore it and, to my horror, my mind returns to my daydream on the beach, to being eaten alive by a group of hungry black men. I quickly finish in Ruben's mouth and then get him off with a few spit-aided pumps of my right hand. He goes to clean up and when he returns I pretend I'm asleep so that he goes back to his own couch.

Ruben is all serious looks and sulky gestures when I find him in the kitchen the next morning. I ignore him and make a Bloody Maria with what remains of the silver tequila. I find Isabelle on the balcony, smoking a long cigarette and drinking a hard cider.

She sees my drink and tips her bottle at me.

"Hair of the dog!" she rasps.

"What's the plan for today?" I ask, staring out at the booming ocean.

"More of the same, really," she says dreamily. "It's supposed to be even hotter, so if you want to run, I'd wait until evening. But not too late—the sun goes down early in Durban."

"Oh great, thanks,"

I hear the deck creak behind me and then get a slap on the back, knocking me towards the deck railing.

I spill some Bloody Maria, leaving bubbly red goo splattered on the deck floor. I whirl around to find Byron holding up a beer and smiling.

"I hear you got some action last night," he says jovially, clinking my glass with his beer.

Oh God.

I take a big gulp of my drink and make a noncommittal noise.

Byron's gaze quickly diverts behind me.

"Look, dolphins!" he yells. Some of the others trot out from inside the cottage to take a better look.

I turn and look out at the frolicking silver beasts playing in the waves. There must be at least fifteen of them.

One of the indistinguishable brunette girls. Tiffany or Tara, or maybe Mara, says, "I'm surprised they're not scared off by the sharks."

I can't hide my surprise. "Sharks? Isn't it too warm for them here?"

She looks at me like I'm insane. "Of course not. They love the warm sea. Some poor surfer just had his arm bit off down in Umhlanga last week. Great White."

I resist laughing at her. Hardly anyone anywhere in the world is attacked by a shark. Just another thing that white South Africans use to tell themselves that the only safe place is behind their own front gates.

I take my drink and sprawl myself across a lounge chair, eager to burn in the sun for a while before anyone is awake enough to try and start a conversation.

✠

I head out at six, sure this will give me enough time to get a run in before it's too dark. I don't even bother to bring a shirt along this time. I catch Ruben's eye on my way out the door and he eyes me hungrily, momentarily forgetting his middle-school approach to flirtation. I smile back despite myself, knowing this will all end horribly but unable to resist the attention.

It's still hot, but without the direct afternoon sun the sea breeze cools my sweat instantly, giving me a nice, stimulating chill as I trot.

The waves are higher, more aggressive, and I'm careful to

stay close to the bluffs. Something about the sideways sunlight and its deeper colors makes the empty beach feel even emptier and melancholy. The white sand seems an alien landscape.

There are no crabs in sight, aside from few carcasses picked clean by sea birds. I envision them buried beneath me, a mass of chitin, segments, and claws writhing just beneath the beach's pristine surface.

I look to the dense bushes on the bluffs for signs of their inhabitance, but I see none. What I do see is a set of low, focused eyes.

I yelp and look closer, but the eyes are gone as quickly as they'd appeared. My fantasy from the day before returns, but now that it feels within the realm of possibility it is horrifying rather than erotic. I consider turning around. I've only run about a mile so far. Not much of a work out, especially considering how much I've been drinking. I think of Ruben's eyes on my body, the attention to how good I look, and decide to soldier on.

I try to put my imagination at bay. Even if I *had* seen eyes in the bushes, surely it is just a vervet or a hadeda or some other African nuisance. It hadn't the murderous eyes of a starving man.

I push harder, moving fast on the packed sand, and quickly reach the point where I'd turned around the day before. The channel has widened, but the water has come back out of the lagoon, allowing me to cross without getting my shoes wet. I continue on, staying on the ocean-side of the lagoon, avoiding the inlets, which are now completely dark and cave-like.

I watch the bushes as I run, and my mind returns to dark corners. What if there is a whole civilization of them in there, waiting for fresh meat to wander by? Fishers of men, waiting and hoping for young, sun-kissed skin to pass, to fall into their trap.

I round another cusp and find yet another uninterrupted beach, another series of inlets smattered with heavy boulders. The boulders create dark, concealed nooks and crannies on the beach and I imagine the hungry men are waiting there too, planning the best way to herd me in.

As I pass one of these rocky nooks, the sheer blackness of it disturbs me. I look up to the horizon and see that the sun has set. *Shit.* Within minutes, it will have dipped below the line of the ocean and I'll have nothing but the stars to guide me.

The path is clear and easy; I'm not worried about getting lost. But being alone in the dark in unknown territory isn't smart.

I turn around and head back towards the cottage. When I round back towards the lagoon, I keep my eyes on the dark inlets on its far side. They must be perfect for sitting and picnicking during the day, hidden in the shade, close enough to the lagoon for frequent warm dips in the salty water. But now, in the dark, they are perfect hiding places. I almost jump when I see a dull glow emanating from one of the far inlets.

My heart thumps in my chest. Squatters on the beach, sitting by a fire, waiting for something to cook.

Stop it. Surely it's just some night fishermen. Or a couple having a romantic picnic.

It's dark now. The moonlight illuminates my sandy path, but the inlets are all black as squid ink aside from the one with the warm light. I can't see who is in it, but the light seems active, pulsing; either it is a fire or someone is moving in front of it.

I keep my eyes glued on the inlet as I run, on full alert, yet I'm still horrified when I see a dark, low shape, hunched and fast, slip from the illuminated inlet into the darkness to its left. The lagoon is to my right, the inlets in a 'U' shape around it, so whatever just came from that inlet has gone in the right direction to cut me off. It's the most direct route to me— going the other way would be much further and the lagoon was still relatively full, too deep for a night swim.

I watch closely and debate turning around. I could try to find someone's house back up the beach. But I'd seen no houses, no signs of civilization. Suddenly, another hunched figure emerges from the inlet, disappearing into the dark before I can ascertain what, or who, it is.

I decide to use my adrenaline to my advantage, to sprint

forward, hopefully passing whoever came from that inlet before they reach me. I pick up my speed, my lungs burning in the sprint.

I leap over the channel that feeds the lagoon. As I approach the juncture of my path and the path that leads around the inlets and around the lagoon, I turn my head, searching the blackness.

I imagine several black warriors emerging from the dark, spears raised. We're near King Shaka's birthplace, that's the only excuse I can think of for jumping to such an image.

My fantasy is interrupted by a real figure's emergence from the darkness. I'm so shocked by my imagined world coming to life that I lose my balance, and fall back, my butt hitting the packed sand with a thud, my legs going up over my neck.

I scuttle like a crab down towards the water, where the moon is reflecting the wet sand, allowing for more visibility. I feel hard pressure on my leg. Not so much pain, but a huge amount of compression followed by wet, loose relief.

I gape down at my leg and see that a large part of my calf is missing. Not missing so much as hanging there, dislodged, torn free and bleeding heavily.

Everything becomes quite clear. So clear, actually, that my first thought is concern over how I managed to be in such a fog just a moment ago. I suddenly see the teeth responsible for my ripped leg, and I hear voices approaching, loud and shrill.

My assailant is not a hunting party of starving men but rather a Rottweiler or some similar breed. He goes in again, this time tearing the flesh of my leg free. I kick out but miss awkwardly.

The Rottweiler is joined by a friend, a similar looking breed. It snarls as it approaches and I roll into the water. I push out, a combination of hopping on one leg and floating. I cut my hands and knees on the rocky ocean floor but I keep pushing outward. I swivel around to see that the dogs are following. Their heads bob above the wave like toothy buoys, their eyes surprisingly friendly for creatures intent on tearing me apart.

Behind them, I hear voices. I see two people running towards the sea, waving their arms. Two white people, their pale skin silver in the moonlight. A woman, adjusting her top, her left breast failing to make it in the first attempt. A man pulling up his shorts.

Panic hasn't set in so much as distance. Getting into the water had been my only goal. Now that the dogs have followed me, I feel as if I am watching this all from a way's off, which is irritating because it seems like a big cliché.

I hear the woman screaming, her voice shrill. She has a big, flat, pale face. Her blonde hair is untethered, billowing in the sea wind.

The man is yelling the dogs' names, I think, but I can't

really tell. But I can hear the woman. She's talking to me. She's screaming in horror and apology.

"They thought you were a *kaffir!*"

One of the dog reaches me, gets my arm. The teeth penetrate, but I manage to pull it free. I push further into the water. My instincts are focused on survival, but every time the woman yells, my brain screams, "*Why is she saying that awful word? She can't say that!*"

Still, I can barely get my head above the water to breathe, let alone scream. I swim further. Adrenaline is making my mind race, competing thoughts paralyzing me. I see the dogs, pacing on shore, snarling, their owners unable to wrangle them. I turn and swim further, reaching deep, dark water.

I don't think that I can be any more afraid but then something brushes my leg and I remember the brunette from the beach house's words, the warning I'd ignored.

Sharks.

GAY ZOO DAY

Christian and I first locked eyes from opposite ends of the London Zoo's kangaroo enclosure, a fire burning between us. This particular fire was caused by neither hearts nor loins but rather by several burning rows of decorative outback grasses, kindled by cigarette butts lazily thrown over the enclosure's balcony by the cocktail-swilling attendees of the zoo's first annual Gay Zoo Day. I noticed Christian because of how still he was, like some kind of jungle cat, which stood out in the undulating crowd. I stared directly at him as the burning went from embery sizzle to hearty yellow flame. He was gorgeous, taller than me, with beautiful blue eyes that he'd accessorized with a dark tan and an eye-matching jewel-blue t-shirt. His hair was buzzed close to his head but shone Weimaraner bronze in the rare London sun. As soon as our eyes met I flashed a toothy smile and wasn't surprised when those baby blues crinkled in interest. A benefit of being an American in London was the natural advantage I gained from a lifetime of fluoride and large orthodontist bills.

Stavros, my closest London friend, spotted Christian just after I did.

"Mine!" he hissed at me and pushed me out of the way, waving like Marilyn Monroe greeting the troops.

It was 2008, and Stavros and I had just gotten our Master's degrees from the London School of Economics, his in something involving public relations and mine in regulation. We'd both moved to London for grad school and subsequently declared it to be home forever. I was from small town America and Stavros from small town Greece, and London was where we felt we belonged—cultured, accepting, and filled with eligible gay bachelors. We were at Gay Zoo Day celebrating the completion of our dissertations and because we'd managed to get jobs in London, no small feat considering the economy. Stavros was starting at a PR firm and I had gotten a fellowship with an advertising conglomerate, WPP.

WPP had made a huge deal out of the statistics of their hires for this fellowship. Out of two thousand applicants they chose only ten, they boasted. Half of one percent. Though I knew the number to be entirely subjective, inflated, and more a matter of taste than one of achievement, it would be lying to say I hadn't started thinking of myself as part of the point five percent.

Stavros was short and slim and had dark, curly, Greek hair, the kind you see on ancient pottery. He smoked a pack of Galois a day, and that had hardened some of the gay out of his voice, which was Greek in accent but tinged with the sounds of a British education, making everything he said sound like a question.

The confidence I'd gained from becoming a point-five-percenter made me feel that I'd reached my most attractive despite having gained the five pounds that everyone gains their first year in England. Okay, ten. I was six-feet tall in my cowboy boots and had dyed my brown hair that copper blonde that foreigners expect American farm boys to have. I did not smoke regularly so my voice, as always, was gay as a daisy.

Stavros and I had gotten dressed that morning at my townhouse in Tower Hill, watching a Celine Dion concert DVD and sharing a bottle of Bacardi while we tried on all of our clothes. Stavros had finally decided that I should wear boot cut jeans, cowboy boots, a blue tank top, and a cardigan in case it rained. Then Stavros decided that he, as always, should wear jeans so tight I had to pull them up for him and a white V-neck that went nipple-low.

I grabbed a box of condoms from my bathroom and stuck several in my back pocket before holding some out for Stavros.

"What are you doing?" he asked, arching a plucked eyebrow. "No one carries those around anymore."

"Of course they do," I said.

"It makes you look like you have AIDS."

I didn't think that he was at all correct but I decided that if I did end up hooking up with a guy, we'd either come back to my place, where I had condoms, or we would go back to his, where surely there would be condoms as well. Despite what Stavros had said, I was pretty sure most people had condoms at home.

"But I saw him first," I whined, though I knew it was a losing battle. In my opinion I was more attractive than Stavros, but he was tenacious: a mongoose stalking cobras.

Christian smiled and waved at both of us, and I contemplated shoving Stavros into the enclosure.

"Look," Stavros whispered to me, "he has a friend! You can have *him*."

The friend, standing behind Christian, had a little bit of a Willem Dafoe thing going on, if you were to sap every bit of sexual energy out of Willem Dafoe. Like Christian, he was tall, but he was hunched in the distinctive stance of a sidekick. I immediately straightened my own shoulders, hoping to avoid anyone thinking that I was Robin to Stavros's Batman.

"Should we go talk to him?" Stavros asked, really asking if

we should play hard to get or if we should just head over and flirt aggressively.

"Let's get a cocktail and see what happens," I told him. This was our motto for most things in life. It allowed for a moment of reflection or a quick reset and, of course, meant more to drink.

While Stavros went to collect our cocktails, however, I made a beeline for Christian. This was a severe violation of our holy friendship code but I knew Stavros would understand if I managed to land a hot guy. When I got to Christian, I was suddenly left wordless. I had no game plan; my only goal had been to beat Stavros to the punch.

Christian smiled and his teeth were so white that in my eyes that did that sparkly *ding!* thing that happens in toothpaste commercials. Obviously he wasn't British.

His eyes wrinkled at the edges when he smiled, and I guessed that he was much older than me. I was twenty-three and would have put him between thirty-five and forty.

"Hi, I'm Christian. You have really pretty eyes."

His accent was German, but, like Stavros's, it had obviously been honed in some wing of British academia. I was thrilled. We were still at that age where sex was as much about collecting as it was pleasure. We counted the number of people we slept with, what countries they came from, and their occupations.

I couldn't think of what to say, my mind clouded by nerves and rum.

Christian took my silence in stride.

"What's your name?" he asked. He didn't move when he spoke and once again he reminded me of a big cat, a mix of leonine stillness and tiger-eyed interest.

"Sam?" I asked, forgetting the question.

"Don't you know?" he said, almost whispered, maintaining eye contact. I had only ever flirted with men around my own age, men who spoke in movie quotes and expressed their desire with fumbling gropes. Christian's intensity already had me in some sort of trance, and I think he knew it.

Christian took it all in stride. Whenever his eyes touched mine I felt nauseous, the rum-addled butterflies in my tummy running into each other and twisting into knots.

He introduced me to Willem, who actual name was Phil. Phil was Christian's roommate. They'd met at the Victoria and Albert Museum, or V&A, where they'd both worked as curators before Christian had taken a gig at some fancy art gallery in Guildhall. My knowledge of curation began and ended with the weird bug guys in *The Silence of the Lambs*, but it seemed like a big deal. I'd not only heard of the V&A, I had visited it often.

After a bit of nervous conversation, Christian seemed to understand that he was going to need to take initiative. "Why don't we get out of here?" he asked. "My place?"

His flat was one of those Narnial places, where an unassuming doorway led you into an alternate world. I had taken to calling apartments *flats* since I had arrived in London, just as I started calling the bathroom *the loo*, culturally appropriating in hopes of building a charming international vocabulary.

The entrance to the flat was down a small alley right off of Chinatown, the kind of alley that gorgeous couples in fashionable raincoats duck into for stolen kisses. We walked up three flights of stairs and then I waited, catching my breath while Christian pulled out his keys. He repeatedly looked over at me, his eyes softening as he saw me, like he was relieved to find me still there. When he opened the door, the first thing I noticed was all of the art in the main hallway, all dark paintings featuring nude men. It all looked very gothic and expensive.

The hallway was the backbone of the flat, with two rooms off of each side and a bathroom straight at the end. Christian told me that the rooms on the left were the kitchen and Phil's bedroom. Phil had stayed at Gay Zoo Day, looking for his own prey.

The first room on the right was a study, three of the walls lined with books, with two comfy-looking chairs sitting back-to-back, bookshop style.

The fourth wall was full of windows that faced the alley,

except that this building was taller than the one it faced, so the windows provided a stunning view of the Westminster area of London, with Big Ben looming above Westminster Abbey and the Houses of Parliament. They were still lit, warm gold-stone-gray, and I felt briefly overwhelmed. I was from a small town in rural Pennsylvania, and my mind's eye still defaulted to that. Then London would unexpectedly reveal its splendor in a moment such as this and I was left utterly dazzled. This was where I was supposed to be. This was home.

The second room on the right was Christian's bedroom, which was the same shape as the study. The left wall was almost entirely taken up by a large, wooden bureau, covered by tiny trinkets and what looked to be jewelry boxes.

The bed was immediately right of the door. It was a king, made up in masculine beige duvet set, and above it, attached to the wall, was a set of wooden bookshelves. I suddenly feared it would fall off and crush us in the night. The books on this shelf seemed more valuable than those in the study, most with leather bindings. I thought of *Anchorman*, as any normal person does when they see leather-bound books.

Christian went to the kitchen to get some wine. There was nowhere to sit so I perched on the end of the bed. I heard a guttural "*Scheiße!*" followed by the clanking of glass and running of water: the distinct sounds of having no clean glasses.

As it seemed Christian would be occupied for a moment, I decided to check out the fancy bookshelf. I slid out of my cowboy boots and socks, quickly bending over to do a smell check on my feet, which were fine. The only way to get close to the bookshelf was to scoot to the head of the bed, stand on my knees, and brace myself against wall or the bottom of the bookshelf itself. I couldn't hope to even guess what the German books were about, but the rest were a mix of classic novels and plays and a few more whimsical books like *The Hobbit,* the first *Harry Potter*, and *The Wind in the Willows.* My eyes were drawn to a beautifully bound copy of *The Jungle Book*, which brought a smile to my face.

Christian came into the room, a glass of wine in each hand, and shut the door with his hip. His eyes ran up and down my body, which was, in yoga terms, in a *receptive* position. I made a move to turn around.

"No. Stay like that," he said.

So there I sat (arched? sun-salutated?) at the head of a very large bed.

"Are all of these books yours?" I asked to fill the quiet. I cringed. Who else's books would be in his bedroom?

He thankfully ignored my stupid question and joined me on the bed. He set one wine glass on the nightstand and crawled slowly up behind me. I felt momentarily smothered by him. He was warmer than I was, taller, his cologne stronger, his hands larger. He engulfed me. Christian pushed my legs apart and scooted his own knees between them. He hand slid his right hand around my waist. His left hand held a glass of wine, but the wine's topaz gleam in the soft bedroom light was outdone by a huge sapphire ring on his ring finger.

He put a wine glass to my lips and placed his head on my shoulder, like he was trying to rest his head on it, but he was too tall and his chin hit my cheek.

I laughed awkwardly and Christian handed me the wine glass, blushing. The hand around my waist quickly found the button of my jeans. He undid it and pulled down the zipper. I felt him back up on the bed and then he had one hand on the bottom of each leg.

"Stretch your legs out straight," he said.

I couldn't remember what underwear I'd worn but I hoped it was something sexy.

"Do you have condoms?" I asked.

His hands stopped in place, my jeans around my ankles.

"I haven't heard that in years," he said, sounding surprised.

"So that's a no?" I tried to sound lighthearted. But didn't everyone have condoms? Maybe Christian was only into oral? Or maybe Stavros hadn't been as full of crap as I'd thought.

"No, but I can run and get some?"

The question was delivered in that questioning way that told me blatantly that he didn't want to go anywhere and he was hoping I'd acquiesce.

I decided to change tactics. I wiggled my rear end at him and said, "There's plenty of fun we can have without con-doms."

He smiled and reached out grabbing me by the waist again. He lost his balance and fell into me. The wine sloshed out and splashed my face and he licked it off while I laughed so hard my stomach hurt.

The next morning I woke up to Christian's lips on my neck. His hips were pressed against my ass and he was rocking slowly.

"You're awfully subtle," I croaked.

I felt him smile into my neck.

I lost myself in the sensation for a moment. Then he pushed, really pushed. How he thought anything of that sort was going to be possible, dry and first thing in the morning, was beyond me. But it was a definite attempt.

"Whoa, sailor," I said, trying to arch my hips forward.

I tried to turn around to face him, but his arms held me in place. I reached behind me and realized that he was *really* turned on. This pleased me greatly, despite the situation.

Still, I needed an escape plan.

"I'm afraid that if I don't go to the loo this second I'm going to pee on you," I said, hoping desperately that wasn't something he was into.

He released me and laughed, "Yuck. Get out of here, heathen."

He slapped me on the butt as I clambered over him. I ran to the bathroom, locked the door behind me, and leaned against it, breathing deeply.

After a moment, Christian yelled, "Did you find it okay?"

I realized the place was so small that of course he would hear me pee. Which was gross, but luckily I had to go anyway, so my fib wasn't entirely a fib.

When I left, I walked southeast from Christian's flat, towards the Thames, and made my way through Leicester Square. It was too early for anyone to be out and about in this part of town, so it was just me and a horde of rough-looking city pigeons, pecking at discarded food and drunkfolk vomit from the night before. It was raining lightly and I skipped through the pigeons. Used to people, they didn't fly off, but rather flapped around my feet like my very own diseased chorus of Disney birds.

There was no agonizing over when Christian would call or when I should call or any of those silly games. He sent me a text that same afternoon, asking me to meet him the next night at the Green Carnation, a new Soho bar with an art deco vibe.

The next evening I took the District Line from Tower Hill down to the Embankment stop, deciding to get off there and enjoy the twenty minute walk north to Soho rather than changing lines. I called Stavros on the walk.

"Hey baby," he answered.

"I'm on my way to drinks with the German. The one I went home with."

I wanted to rub it in a little bit.

I told him about my night with Christian. He sensed my apprehension over the condoms and decided to get straight to the point.

"I told you, no one uses condoms anymore," Stavros said casually. "And there's that gay morning after pill. If you think you've caught HIV, you can go to the hospital the next morning, and they give you pills to wipe it out."

"Stavros! That is not a real thing. I would have heard if they'd cured AIDS."

"It's real. Emmanuel did it. You just go to the hospital and say you were accidentally exposed and they'll treat you."

"No way. Why doesn't everyone use it?"

"Everyone does! You're just out of touch!"

"Everyone does not. Why aren't they giving it to people in Africa?"

"I mean *everyone* as in *Europeans*. Of course they aren't giving it to Africans. There probably isn't enough."

"Okay, we need to have a conversation about your views on Africa. But later. I don't have time right now."

"If you trust him, you can ask him. Do you trust him?" Stavros asked.

"No. Yes. I don't know. How could I know? We've only spent one night together."

"Well, you trusted him enough to go home with him."

We both laughed at that.

Stavros turned serious. "Sometimes you just know. Do you want to date him?"

"Of course I do," I said automatically, surprising myself. "He's hot, he's smart. At least I think he's smart. He didn't actually talk a lot. But he has a lot of books that smart people have. And we have such a great story. We met at the zoo!"

"Yes, after you betrayed your friend to get him. Great story. Go get him. Talk about dating. Call me later."

"That is *horrible* advice. I'm not going to talk about dating. What *should* I talk about?"

"Just get a cocktail and see what happens."

"That doesn't work for everything!"

"Talk about sex. Then he'll want to have sex. Then you'll have sex."

"Oh, God. Bye."

This time, we lay side by side on his bed, naked, and drank wine. It was nice not to rush things.

"Do you know why I want this to work?" he asked as we lay there.

"Why?" I asked, butterflies bouncing in my stomach.

"Because we have such a story. Meeting at the zoo, walking home under the moon, our first night."

The thickness of his accent made this sound even cornier, but I couldn't help but smile. Hadn't I just said the same thing to Stavros?

I really liked Christian. And despite the awkward moments of the first night, I began to feel like perhaps I really did trust him.

"What's your status?" I asked, uncomfortably using the casual terminology for AIDS status. After I blurted it out I thought that perhaps I could have transitioned into the question a bit more smoothly.

"Don't you think it's a bit early on to talk about things like that?" he said. Hadn't he just said that he wanted this to work? And when *was* a good time to talk about status? *Which anniversary is the AIDS anniversary, Christian? After herpes, before silver?*

I looked over at him, eager to see his face and understand his mood, but he was turned away from me. I took a sip of wine. I watched his back as he sighed heavily and reached over to the nightstand and pulled out a small paper bag. He rolled back over and theatrically pulled out a pack of Trojans and some KY.

"Is this what you want?" he asked, and smiled again.

I smiled back.

"Yes," I said, maybe a little too enthusiastically. "Right now."

I gulped the rest of my wine and handed him the glass. I was still a bit uneasy, but if we had protection I was willing to have the whole status talk another time.

I considered what position I should get in. I figured that on my back would be the place to start, but Christian had other ideas.

"Turn over," he said. It wasn't a command, but it wasn't a question either.

"Sure," I said. "Like on my knees, or flat?"

"Flat."

He grabbed a pillow from the top of the bed.

"Lift your hips." Again, no questions.

I lifted my hips and he shoved the pillow under me in one swift motion.

"Condom!" I reminded him, proud of myself for sticking to my guns.

I heard a foily rip and plasticine crinkle and then, once again, Christian engulfed me. I didn't even get a "brace yourself!" He completely covered me on the bed and though he was holding himself up with his arms, which were caged around either side of my ribs, the weight of his lower body against mine felt almost too heavy to bear. He kissed me on the back and started moving in heavy, weighty strikes. The angle and the pace were off. I tried to move, to get comfortable, but I was completely pinned in place.

I didn't feel as if there was any consideration on his part as to whether or not I was enjoying the experience. He made no move to touch me, to change his pace or his angle. Irritated, I put my hands palm down on the bed and pushed up—like I was doing a push-up. This interrupted his rhythm and though he continued thrusting, he pulled his arms up, taking a moment to stretch them. I turned my head, hoping to catch his eye and establish some sort of connection with him, to dial up the passion, but he was looking down. I followed his gaze; to his right was an open, unused condom. Why would there be an unused condom just lying there? Had he torn one?

No. He'd never put it on.

Christian brought his head up and I turned my head back around sharply, as if I had been the one caught doing something wrong. He leaned in and kissed me between the shoulder blades and then put his hand there, right where he'd kissed me, and pushed. The pressure caused my arms to buckle and he caged me in once again. I found myself unable to speak. I knew that I should say *stop*. It was on the tip of my tongue.

Absurdly, my mind was invaded by the consideration of how fragile a relationship is at the very start, on the second date. The slightest misunderstanding could end things entirely.

I wondered if I was mistaken. Maybe he'd opened a condom, ripped it accidentally, and put on another.

He had seen me see him. Surely he would have felt the need to explain himself if he'd just gone and abandoned the condom?

My cheek was pressed against the bedspread and I couldn't turn my head far enough to fully see him. I couldn't get enough traction with the duvet to hoist myself back up.

I was shocked by my own lack of will. I felt the need to say something, to do something quickly, but I didn't have the words. Was there a gentle way to suggest a brief break, an opportunity to suggest that he put on a condom? I wanted to say something that would make it clear that I knew what he'd done but that I was giving him a second chance.

Then he finished.

I hadn't had enough time. I wasn't done thinking about how to get out of it. I had never had unprotected sex before. Now I had. The evidence was clear and my hope that I'd been seeing things, that he really had been wearing a condom, was crushed.

Laying there with his breath on my back, I thought of those *National Geographic* videos that show lions chasing down wildebeests on the Savanna. When a lion gets a wildebeest, it goes completely limp, frozen, laying in the lion's grip. I always wondered why they didn't move. Now I knew.

Christian wordlessly lifted himself off of me and went to the bathroom. I heard him in the shower and a switch flipped within me. I may not have managed to get away during the act, but I sure as hell wasn't going to stick around now. I quickly gathered my clothes from the floor and pulled them on. Then something caught my eye; Christian's beautiful sapphire ring, sitting right there on the bureau next to his wallet and a pair of reading glasses.

I thought about taking the ring. Not to wear, but because I

felt that somehow it might even the playing field. Make it a trade rather than a theft.

But I knew that taking the ring would mean seeing Christian again. And I already knew that I didn't want that. So I left the ring where it was and ran to the door. As I ran down the stairs and burst out into the alley, my cruel mind dragged me back to our conversation just a little bit before, when Christian had evaded my question about his status. Cold reality broke out all over my face, sucking the heat out of my hands. What if Christian had AIDS? He'd avoided our status talk.

Suddenly, Stavros's voice rang out from my memory, my gay, Greek, fairy godmother: And there's that gay morning after pill. If you think you've caught HIV, you can go to the hospital the next morning, and they give you pills to wipe it out.

I needed to get to a hospital. But what could I say? How could I explain that I hadn't wanted to have unprotected sex but that I'd done nothing to stop it?

I caught a cab to St. Thomas' Hospital, which was just over the Westminster Bridge on the south side of the Thames. I looked back across the river before going through the doors, looking for the major London landmarks. The lights were now out on most of them and I stared at their dark forms, in reverse of how I'd seen them from Christian's window.

The doctor came to see me while I sat there on a cold metal table, my clothes replaced by a thin green robe. My fear of having to explain myself was unfounded; she calmly and respectfully told me that she would put me on Post-Exposure-Prophylaxis, or PEP. It was a month-long course of medication that, if started within seventy-two hours of exposure and adhered to rigorously, could prevent HIV infection.

I asked the doctor how effective it was and she told me with clear-eyed directness that it was hard to measure because in most studies the patients were not entirely sure of whether or not their partners were HIV positive to begin with and that it was also an intense course of drugs, one that must be completed in order for it to work, so there was a significant drop off rate. But, with all of those factors considered, it looked to be about eighty percent effective.

I did the math. I was forty times more likely to get HIV than I had been to get my job, which up to that point had been the most important percentage in my life.

I agreed to the drugs.

The doctor then got into specifics. It was three pills, taken every twelve hours. Missing a dose was not an option. Legally, she could only give me two doses. I'd have to go to the HIV/AIDS Clinic on the sixth floor of the hospital the next day to get the full course of treatment.

Me? Go to the AIDS clinic? With the people who have AIDS?

The doctor's final words to me were about how lucky I was. I scoffed, but then she told me that in America they only offered PEP to police and medical professionals. And in most countries, they didn't offer it at all.

Though they made me horribly nauseous, the two small white pills were easy to take. The real problem was the big yellow pill. It was Lego-sized and mustard colored, like a button in a seventies sci-fi movie or the pad of a witch's thumb.

The effect of the pills on my mind and body were severe and instantaneous. I was always tired, suffered from terrible stomach pains and headaches, and could not concentrate. I bloated up and stayed that way, my skin stretched thin. The only things I could stand to eat were white bread and boiled chicken.

Still, I told no one. All that anyone would hear would be *AIDS*. At work, I'd be the new guy being treated for AIDS. My friends would tell their other friends and soon I'd be that guy with AIDS, before I even knew if I had it. My parents would want me to come back to Pennsylvania.

In truth, I felt as if I already had the disease. I became obsessed with my twenty percent chance. I was in the point five percent. Twenty percent was a sentence, a certainty.

When I tried to tell myself that it would be a twenty percent chance *only* if Christian was definitely HIV positive and
if the disease had in fact been absorbed into my system, I felt
as if I was making excuses to avoid the inevitable. False op-
timism. It was a twenty percent chance of death.

I went to the HIV/AIDS clinic twice a week for four weeks so
they could monitor my progress as I took the pills. The PEP
was so strong that in many patients it caused liver and kid-
ney damage. So they had to look at that. And they needed to
make sure that I didn't have a "super strain" of HIV, one that
could appear early and could signal increased danger to the
city at large.

Each time I arrived at the hospital I took the elevator to
the seventh floor and then walked down a flight of stairs, just
so that no one would see me hit the button for the AIDS floor.
There were counselors at the clinic specifically for gay patients. Mine was Charles, a distant polar bear of a man who I
had to see twice weekly during my twenty-eight days of
treatment and then once every other week for the following
six months. The clinic needed to monitor my organs and to
check for that potential super strain. Also, they wouldn't be
able to see if the PEP had worked for six months, at which

point I would either be given a clean bill of health or begin my real, big boy HIV treatments.

I usually met with Charles right after I'd peed in a cup and had my blood taken. He would quickly ask about my feelings and then hand me a paw full of condoms and lube packets and send me on my way.

There was apparently some strategy to these visits, because when my six months were over Charles was the one elected to deliver my results. It was one of London's rare snowy days, bleak and wet and gray, two days after Valentine's Day. I was so nervous that I threw up over the side of the Westminster Bridge on my walk to the hospital, in full view of Parliament. Once I'd had the blood test and peed in the cup, they moved me back to the waiting room to wait for my results. I sat there counting the AIDS sores on the faces of the other men in the room. I was taken back to the pigeons of Leicester Square that morning after my first night with Christian. And now, months later, here they were again, my diseased chorus, now a group of sore-marked men.

I wanted to jump up on my chair and scream, "I'm not like you! I didn't make this choice. Someone did this *to* me!"

I felt like the punch line of some joke about what the city does to naïve little boys.

Finally Charles came out and called me back. I suppose the clinic hoped that he and I would have built a trust by now, that I would be happy that he was the one delivering the news of my fate. But I hated him. I hated everyone.

He sat at his desk. Slowly looking through paperwork as if this wasn't a defining moment in my life. Or maybe he got off on diminishing it.

He looked up, looked me in the eye for what must have been the first time ever, and said, "All clear." He grabbed some condoms and lube from the bowl on his desk and dropped them in front of me. "Make sure to use protection."

I burst into tears. Not tears of vindication. Angry, desperate, gasping tears. Tears of getting out of jail free, of dodging a bullet.

Charles' face didn't soften. He passed me his card and said, "No need for you to come back here. But give me a call sometime. I'll take good care of you."

In some horrible twist of fate, Phil and I emerged from the back of the clinic into the waiting room at the same time. In six months I had never seen anyone I knew, and then, with snot flowing and a tear-raw face, I ran into the second-to-last person I wanted to see. It felt too convenient in a city of eight million, but we were at the closest clinic to Soho, so it wasn't exactly an "It's a Small World" moment.

Phil looked even creepier than he had all of those months before. His face was so sunken that it the drawn-on look of a salamander's. And still some Willem Dafoe. There was a round black sore on his forehead. I wondered if I could ask him if Christian was sick, too.

What if he'd given it to Christian? Did they sleep together? The thought made me burn with anger and jealousy.

His expression was smug. "Sam, funny seeing you here."

I faked a smile, wiped snot from under my nose. "Hi, Phil."

Phil stared at me expectantly. "You look rough. Want to get a cup of coffee? I'll buy."

No, I didn't want to get a cup of coffee with Phil. But it would be a good deed. Probably Phil didn't get to have a lot of coffee with handsome men. And I was curious. Was I curious about whether Christian was actually sick? Yes. But also, did he miss me? Was he sorry?

We had coffee at a Cafe Nero directly across Westminster Bridge Road from the hospital entrance. The interior was a miasma of Valentine's Day decorations. I couldn't have felt any less love for Phil. I sipped a peppermint mocha, thinking that I should be drinking champagne to rejoice in my health. Cold, tired relief ran through my veins. I wanted to sleep for a thousand years, to wake up having forgotten everything from Gay Zoo Day onward. Shouldn't I have learned something from it? Maybe sometimes it is enough to escape.

Phil was blunt. As soon as we were seated, he asked, "So, why the tears?"

I wondered if he knew Christian's side of the story. I wonder if Christian *had* a side of the story.

"AIDS scare. I was on the PEP, and they just gave me a clean bill of health."

He raised one of his gobliny eyebrows. "Was it a surprise? The clean bill of health? If you catch it in time, I hear that PEP stuff is pretty effective. I wish I would have had the chance."

I knew he was looking for sympathy, that he wanted me to ask him how it had happened for him. But I didn't.

"It's only eighty percent effective. When I had the scare, I'd just gotten this job where they'd only hired half of one percent of applicants. And I'd gotten into my head that I was special, you know? That if I was in the point five percent for the one thing, how could I not be in the twenty percent for the other? I thought that maybe it was my destiny, that I was meant to get sick somehow. So when I heard I wasn't, it was just such a shock. I'd been living like I had AIDS."

I hadn't told anyone this, and I'm not sure why I felt compelled to tell Phil. Maybe because I didn't care what he thought. Maybe because I thought maybe he'd tell Christian.

I smiled down at my mug and looked up at Phil, whose salamander-face had warped into something even more vicious. When he spoke, it was a spit-filled hiss.

"You're such a fucking idiot."

"What?" I choked out, shocked.

"You know it's HIV, not AIDS, that you were being tested for. And HIV will get you for lots of things. It will get you if you're black, it will get you if you're white. It will get you if you're a man, it will get you if you're a woman. It will get you if you're poor—*especially* if you're poor. You know when it got me? My first time."

Phil's anger was increasing with his rant and I felt pinned down by it. It seemed disproportionately angry; we barely knew each other. The part of me that wasn't shocked wanted to roll my eyes. This was one of those speeches enabled by the Internet age. He'd probably typed the same thing on someone else's MySpace profile.

He continued, "But it won't get you because you're fucking special. HIV has never gotten someone because they were so damned special that it just had to get them. Fuck you."

"You don't even know me," I said, trying to sound firm, but it came out pinched.

"I thought I'd heard everything, but you being so *special* that you were destined for HIV is just the absolute best. You get fucked bareback and suddenly you're a martyr. Thank

God for the rest of us you didn't get it. You'd be at the front of the fucking parade."

I wanted to fight back, to tell him how wrong he was, to slap him across the face. I wanted to tell him to go and get on one of those soapboxes in Hyde Park and yell at someone who would listen. But I couldn't. So I just stood up and walked out the door, managing to keep the tears in until I stepped out into the dirty London snow.

Because we'd set it on fire the previous year, the kangaroo enclosure was off limits for the London Zoo's second annual Gay Zoo Day. We gathered instead in the Reptile House, where the animals were protected from the swarm of vodka-guzzling men by thick layers of glass.

"I can't believe it's your last week in London," Stavros said for the millionth time.

"I can," said Joe, Stavros's boyfriend of four months, who hated my guts. Joe was Irish and had the body of a leprechaun and the face of an ostrich.

"I'll visit all the time," I said. "I'll fly British Airways from Johannesburg and stop in London on the way to everywhere."

I was leaving London for South Africa. It was for work, though I'd asked for the transfer.

"All of those African men! It's like you're winning the lottery," Stavros fanned himself at the thought, drawing a glare from Joe. "But be careful."

"Careful of what?"

"You know," Stavros said, shooting me a knowing look. "There is so much AIDS around. Use protection."

After I'd gotten my final test results, I'd finally told Stavros about what had happened with Christian. Even though his "morning after" pill had worked, he'd changed his tune, at least to me, always reminding me to use protection.

Still, I couldn't give him a complete pass.

"That's rich coming from you. Didn't you once tell me that 'no one uses condoms anymore'?"

Joe looked like he'd swallowed a pincushion.

Stavros glared at me but then froze, looking past me.

"Don't turn around," he whispered.

Naturally, I turned around, only to see Christian over by the pythons. One of those very pythons had been in the *Harry Potter* movie. If only I could make the glass disappear and knock him in. How Freudian it would be if I killed Christian with a snake?

He was talking to some young guy, a pale ginger with a slim waist and a big butt. I wondered if they were together and felt that familiar surge of jealousy in my chest.

"Turn around," Stavros hissed.

I turned back to face him. Joe was looking at Stavros, his eyes questioning, and Stavros sent him off to get cocktails.

"You've got him whipped," I said.

Stavros smiled. "I've got skills. Anyways, I'll spy on the German. If he sees you, he might want to talk, and one of us will have to kill him. And I don't want to get kicked out until we've used all of our drink tickets."

He had a point.

"Okay, fine. Does he look sick? Sores, weight loss, weight gain, track marks?"

Stavros squinted his eyes under his bushy eyebrows.

"No, he looks healthy. But his tan looks really fake."

I considered, and not for the first time, that I'd been wrong about all of it. That I'd overreacted. That Christian hadn't been sick and thus removing the condom hadn't been risky at all. But over time I had realized that the HIV wasn't the point. If anything, the PEP had been some kind of warped blessing, though I'd never say that to anyone suffering from the disease. But my experience had finally forced me to get educated about HIV and AIDS, about treatment, and about my own unfortunate prejudices. The point, at least when it came to Christian and me, was the deception.

I tried to turn my hurt into something more altruistic, if only to save face with Stavros. "What about that other guy? Should we say something to him? Warn him?"

After continuing to stare for a moment, Stavros said, "I think it's too late to warn him," and then turned his eyes on me, looking concerned.

"What do you mean?"

I spun around again. Christian and the redhead were kissing. I thought that was what Stavros was referring to, but then I saw the redhead's sparkling ring finger, stretched across Christian's face as he gripped it for the kiss.

Christian's giant blue ring looked even bigger on the redhead's smaller hand.

I watched for another moment, dumbfounded, and when they pulled away from one another and turned to meet some friends I saw that Christian had a simple silver band on his own ring finger. Their group chatted, exchanging European cheek kisses and handshakes before walking off together in the direction of the bar.

I turned back to Stavros, who reached out for a hug. I hugged him fiercely and started to cry into his shoulder. I was trying to be angry, to be outraged. Which I was. But I was also jealous. I wanted to go back and see where it would have gone. I wanted to go back and force him to wear a condom. To yell at him and have him make it up to me with jewelry.

Joe returned and handed us drinks, sensitive enough to keep his mouth shut as I had my meltdown. Then, after a few moments of wallowing, I downed my drink in a gulp and gave Stavros a kiss on the cheek.

"Should we go somewhere else?" Stavros asked. "We can leave if you want."

But I didn't want to leave. This was our last time out together. We were celebrating a year at our jobs, Stavros's continued love of London, and my new adventure in Africa. Secretly, we were toasting my health and looking for someone for Stavros to replace Joe with.

I smiled at him and shook my head no.

"Let's get a cocktail and see what happens."

THE SELF-BANISHED

✝

Jumonville

The Methodist church camp at Jumonville, just south of Pittsburgh, is famous for the big white cross that sits atop Dunbar's Knob, Jumonville's highest hill. At least one visit to the cross is a requirement of every camper's Jumonville experience. The cross, known in Jumonville as The Great Cross of Christ, is sixty feet tall and made of several hundred tons of metal and concrete, a rather aggressive interpretation of the humbly man-sized cedar, pine, and cypress of the True Cross. Years ago, a group of fifteen boys took their requisite pilgrimage to The Great Cross of Christ, a brief detour from a week of fishing camp. Their leader, Big Jim, a retired pastor with multiple sclerosis and a passion for bass fishing, led them by lantern light to the top of Dunbar's Knob, struggling greatly over the vines and ferns and rocks on the path to Dunbar's bulbous zenith but trusting God to give him the strength and vision to get them to the top. Under the cross's mighty metal wings, Big Jim prayed with the boys and then taught them one of his favorite hymns. "Shut de doh!" he sang to them. "Shut the door!" they quacked back. "No, children, it's a spiritual. Sing it like the Africans!" So, on their descent, the fifteen chalk-white Pennsylvania boys sang "Shut de doh, keep out de devil, shut de doh, keep the devil in da night!" Despite being cacophonously off-key, the hymn strengthened them, made them less afraid of the dark. One of the boys, Chris, a brooding fourteen-year-old whose parents had sent him to fishing camp to make friends or find the Lord, vowed to learn more about Africans, because he was pretty sure they hadn't written this awful song. Another of the boys, Dakota, was talkative and energetic and could think about nothing but Chris and occasionally the glory of God. On their dark descent down Dunbar's Knob, Dakota threw his glasses in the dirt and crunched them under his foot. "Shit," he yelped when Chris was within earshot. "I broke my glasses and can't see anything." He couldn't see Chris smile in the dark, but he did hear him say, "No one can see us, so grab my hand and I'll lead you down."

Dakota

I am a Scrubbing Bubble. Mary Poppins, Mr. Clean, those people who help the hoarders on television, Alice from *The Brady Bunch* with a dash of Suze Orman. Today, that's who I am. Normally, I'm the kind of guy who spends thirty minutes of every hour overwhelmed by choice. But today, I have singular focus. I fluff pillows, clean dishes, throw cinnamon buns into our rarely used, state-of-the-art General Electric oven. For the smell, not the taste. I find that Robby has stashed some pot in his usual spot, the magazine holder by his recliner. I grind it up in the garbage disposal. I empty all of our liquor bottles and throw the fallen soldiers into the trunk of my car. In a moment of inspiration, I run to our bedside table. I shake the lowest drawer and hear old sex toys clickety-clack together in the back like mismatched silverware. I throw those in the car as well and I quickly call Robby to tell him that I'm shoving multiple dildos in my trunk but when I call I hear the tornado beats of Robby's Beyoncé ringtone and realize he's left his phone at home. Surely he will come back and get it; Robby is never away from his phone. And today, of all days, to be out of touch. We have a social worker coming to inspect us, to look in our drawers and in our bank accounts and into our hearts and minds and marriage. To see if we're responsible enough, normal enough, to have a baby. And I can't reach him. Of course he'll come back for it. I consider taking it to him at the school, but he doesn't like it when I show up during class. "Look at the gym teacher's gay husband!" he thinks they'll giggle, forgetting that everyone in this small town already knows everything about us. I pick up his phone. He always says it's a betrayal for us to check each others' phones or emails. I say I don't mind, I've got nothing to hide. He says it's just as bad as cheating. But since he's left me alone to clean up our house and our lives I figure I can cheat just this once.

Chris

I turn on the small fan in my office, which is about the size and style of a spaceship escape pod from a 70s sci-fi movie. Sana'a is usually hot. The embassy's air conditioning is down again. Nothing here ever works for long. That applies to the appliances and the people. Our security team is outsourced, basically soldiers-for-hire, their allegiance to dollar signs. The rest of us are here because of low rank or high pay or some combination of the two. The U. S. of A. pays us more to work where we might die, and if no one volunteers they start at the bottom of the list. I had the luxury of being the low man on the totem pole *and* not giving a fuck where they sent me. I walk down the beige-tiled hallway to the front desk. Zarina will have gotten more contraband liquor over the weekend and if I flirt with her she'll give me first pick. In Yemen you can drink in the comfort of your own home but good luck finding any to buy. I brought some in my luggage, which they couldn't search—thank you diplomatic pass- port—but that's long gone. I round the corner, the yellow and white tiles on the wall reminding me of *Dawn of the Dead.* Most of the backwater embassies look like this. Like the US was an alien race that colonized the world in the 1970s and then disappeared forever. I see Zarina gathering the mail in her soft arms. I don't recognize the mail guy, but he looks like he's having a rough day. Zarina grips a package wrapped in brown paper and I see the mail guy wince. I barely have time to think "oh fuck" and the package explodes, blossoming like a big orange flower, burying Zarina and the mail guy and the other desk staff, throwing me into those fucking yellow tiles.

Jumonville

The cicadas sang their shrill song as Chris led Dakota down the hill, sounding far better than the group of boys attempting a spiritual. Chris deftly moved Dakota around trees and through bushes, staying far enough behind Big Jim and the other boys so that they couldn't see but close enough that they could answer if the others called for them. Both boys were silent, and both could only feel their hands, conscious of every millimeter of flesh. Dakota's mind raced, he wanted to say everything, "I like you." "I'm gay." "I'm not gay." "You have really nice teeth." "Can I kiss you?" Chris kept his mind blank, wallowing in sensation, the warmth of their hands together, the stretching feeling from his lungs down to his belly, the smile pulling at his lips. He could hear Dakota breathing heavily in the dark and wondered if he was afraid. He rubbed his thumb against the other boy's palm to comfort him. Dakota wondered if the rubbing was a signal of some kind. He looked back over his shoulder to The Great Cross of Christ looming above them, its white metal glowing in the moonlight, and thought that surely God was acting through Chris's hand. Before he had time to second guess his thoughts, Dakota yanked Chris's arm like a garden hose, pulling the other boy towards him. He let the Lord lead his lips and they landed right on Chris's, which, and this surprised both of them, parted in a smile and kissed back.

Dakota

I punch the pass code into Robby's phone, which is 0-0-0-0 because he has the short-term memory of a sea horse. At our wedding, I delivered a lengthy list of how we met (in college), how we both wanted the same things (small town life, children), how we were strong in our faith (even if the church didn't want us), and how I was his forever. He forgot his vows and responded with "I agree." I check the web browser on his phone and find the history cleared. I open the text messages and scroll down, recognizing all of the names. Down the list: me, his best friend Diane, his mother, his brother, my mother, Diane H., then more family and colleagues. I look at the list again. Diane is saved as Diane *and* Diane H. I don't think Robby knows two Dianes, so I open the Diane H. message.

Diane: I can't believe how fat Maureen got!

Robby: He was so hot in school how could he marry Maureen?

Nothing too suspicious there, though I'm moderately outraged that he called another guy hot. But there are no crimes of the mind. We've been together since we were nineteen, it would be crazy for him not to *wonder* after ten years. We were each others' first. Well, not my first kiss. That was Chris Thompson. Thinking about Chris still makes me feel all fuzzy. The dark night, warm air, his hand in the dark. How can I remember something so vividly fifteen years later? I scroll back up to the first Diane message on the phone. It's from earlier this morning, three o'clock. Why would Diane be texting at three in the morning? I open the message.

Robby: Fuck fuck fuck!

I scroll down.

Diane: I've wiped the server, don't worry about it.

Robby: What the hell do you mean they arrested him?

Diane: Listen, dude, they arrested him this morning and they have to have his server. Clear your computer. I wiped it from my end but you don't want the files hanging around.

I don't understand what Robby and Diane were talking about. I scroll down further. It isn't Diane, of course. Then, three days ago:

Robby: That's fucking hot.

Diane: My guy has a new server. Will send you details. Look at this. Don't worry, it's encrypted.

And there's a video clip. I press it, not thinking. I can't figure it out at first; it's like staring at a watercolor up close. Then I see. Flesh against flesh. Adult flesh against young flesh. Very young flesh. I scream, fling the phone like it bit me, but its venom still festers in the wound.

Chris

My ears ring. My face is burnt but I can't detect any significant injuries. I'm on the floor. I blacked out briefly but my mind knows that not much time has passed. I am fully aware of everything that has happened, so I doubt a concussion. I pull myself up. I look around for injured colleagues but they are all quite obviously dead. The front of the building has blown open. Through the smoke I see the front lawn and the gate. A truck, it's front end reinforced with sloppily coiled, rusted metal, has barreled through the front gate. No security guards in sight. The truck must have just gotten through because the doors are only just now starting to open. Of course, they lead with their guns, and I catch only a glimpse of ski-masked faces before I turn and run back the hallway. My hearing slowly returns, though everything sounds tinny. The lights have gone out, emergency lights illuminating portions of wall and floor. Suddenly, I'm in *Alien*, running for my life through a 1970s vision of the future. As I wind my way through the dark a song comes into my head, and I hum "Shut de doh, keep out de devil. Shut de do, keep de devil in da night." Despite my circumstances, probably because of the adrenaline, I laugh. This can't be the last song I think of. But the song leads to a memory of a warm hand in the dark. Not a repressed memory—I think of it often. But instead of shame, I feel regret. That's a change. I know I need to get to the safe haven, which is supposedly fireproof and bulletproof. Given that it was installed by the same security contractors who apparently abandoned the gate, I have little confidence. That room has documents that I need to shred and a gun cabinet. I round the corner and see two men, bushy beards sticking out below their masks, dumping gasoline liberally into the hallway. If they'd come from the front they'd had to have gone past me so there must be multiple entry points. Or it's an inside job. I hear them barking at each other, thinking I'm going to need to translate. But they're British. And young. New recruits. Still, I wait for them to say something about Allah, but they just complain about how they hadn't seen enough action and then strike a match. I'm disappointed, because I'd have some kind of respect for them if they were doing this for God.

Jumonville

They had to stop kissing, worried that if they fell too far behind the other campers would come looking. But to Dakota it felt like the start of something special. In his mind he imagined them commuting between their small towns, telling their parents that they were best friends. Then when they turned sixteen they'd be able to drive back and forth to see each other. They could go to the prom together and then the same college. Or they could head out, travel the world. Chris focused on the feel of Dakota's hand, ignoring the heat in his own cheeks, the shakiness in his knees. The real world, and the shame that came with it, threatened to break through and he pushed it back. He knew it would come later, so he tried to think of nothing but the moment, the dirt below his feet, the cross on the hill, the hand holding onto his in the dark night.

Dakota

I've often fantasized about Robby cheating on me. I'd discover a text on his phone, or come home to find him in bed with the UPS man, and I would slap him across the face and blaze through the house, a comet of righteous anger, packing my things into a suitcase, putting them in his car (it's nicer than mine), and driving away to a new life. But this wasn't cheating. A small part of me rejoices in being disgusted at what I had seen. If society tells you you're a pervert long enough you maybe start to wonder. Now I feel like I am a good person. And Robby isn't. I wonder if it's been planted. Or maybe it's spam. Like a virus, that sends stuff like that to your phone and then pretends to respond as you. Am I in denial? Robby and I have been together forever, how would I have not noticed this? Why would he leave his phone here if he had this kind of thing to hide? He does have a lot on his mind, with the social worker visiting and apparently a computer full of illegal hell-porn to erase. If Robby is caught, we'll never get a baby. Even if I divorce him, they will still see that I was married to him, someone who did something so horrible. There's no way I can fix this, hide it, clean it up. I have built my whole life around having a family, children. I wanted to travel, but we have saved every penny since college for a house and for adoption. To show everyone, to have a normal life, a small-town American life. No, I've put myself in the position to lose everything because of someone else's crimes. Checkmate, but I was playing against myself. I pray. I pray and I pray and then I think of the last time I prayed so hard. Suddenly I'm under The Great Cross of Christ praying for Chris Thompson to notice me. It worked that time, didn't it? But now that I've thought about it, as hard as I try, I can't pray to fix the present. Instead I pray to be back on that hill in the dark, being led by the hand in the warm summer night.

Chris

One of them takes off his mask and his pale face glows bone white in the emergency lighting. I smile, hoping that a security camera picks this up and that all of the raving loons at home will see that terrorists come in all colors. If this isn't covered up once we're all dead. I follow protocol, retreat, and wind through a back hallway towards the safe haven. This way will take longer, precious time I do not have. Still, I follow the rules. The one time I broke them, a weak moment in Dubai, I got myself arrested for "homosexual acts" and had to use my diplomatic immunity to get myself home. Perfect record tarnished, moved to a desk, put on the bottom of the list. No one else cared about the homo part, just the getting arrested part. I was the one who cared about the homo part. I take these posts in countries where doing those things is illegal because I know that will keep me from acting on my urges. I built a career keeping the devil in me at bay. Smoke has started to gather at the ceiling. As I move slowly down the hallway, the smoky curtain darkens and moves down the wall. I try to think of myself as Roger Moore in a shark tank, water rising. For some reason, I think again to Dakota, his hand, his lips. Out of all of my memories, achievements, degrees, family, this is what I'm thinking about now? But the image gathers behind my eyes, a window for me to step through. The smoke on my burnt face becomes the warm

Jumonville night, the whirring of the alarms those cicadas. I hold my young mind at bay, the first and last time I remember doing so, as Dakota's lips meet mine, and it feels like a discovery, the first of many times that this kind of thing will happen, the secret that adults keep from children. This is the last thing I want to think about.

THE CHRISTMAS CARD

"Picca, darling, the Christmas card isn't really a big deal, is it?" Charles asked her, wiping powdered sugar from his mustache.

Picca narrowed her eyes over the mother-of-pearl frames of her reading glasses and captured her husband with her glare.

"Yes, my love, the Christmas card is a *very* big deal."

Picca found Charles' trivializing of something so dear to her heart to be thoughtless. She had spent the previous ten minutes telling him her plan for a Christmas card that would finally trump whatever it was that her sister Fleur chose to commission this year.

Fleur's Christmas cards were not bought. Nor were they found, crafted, or even bespoke. Every year, Fleur's famous Christmas cards were *commissioned*, according to Fleur.

Even if Fleur commissioned something so stunning this year that it made their overlapping Rolodexes of customers believe she'd dug up Van Gogh and pushed a paintbrush into his boney hand, Picca's card would certainly make more of an impression. And she wanted Charles to share her enthusiasm for it. Wasn't that what their marriage was about? If nothing else, their marriage was a shared plan.

She tried a different approach. She softened her face from a glare to a look of blank feminine interest.

"Sweetheart, aren't you at least excited to use that divine camera I just bought you?"

Just last month, September, Picca had driven up to Rochester to pick up the camera personally. It was a Canon EOS 6D something-or-other, the best of the best according to *Consumer Reports*. The trees had been in full autumn bloom then, marching vibrantly towards death. The fiery hues of the sugar maples in particular dazzled Picca. She felt kindred to them. It had taken her a long time, almost a lifetime, to feel a part of this place. Unlike the rest of her family, who put their names on vineyards and stables as if they were anything more than opportunistic land-grabbers.

Picca had always felt special, *more* special than where she was from, than *whom* she was from. She'd never been able to put a finger on precisely why, but she knew it in her bones.

Over time she had grown to appreciate this place of blazing trees and sweet grapes and cold blue water. And Picca finally felt like she was part of the landscape, like the sugar maples, beautiful and strong but also marching towards an inevitable conclusion.

"Yes, yes, of course I am. It's a great piece of technology, that camera. I just don't want you to be disappointed, dear," Charles said. He took a sip of mulled cider and smiled at her.

You don't want me to be disappointed? Can you go back in time?

The smell of the cider burnt her heart, the nostalgia almost too much to bear. Her mother had put out a plate of powdered-sugar-covered cake donuts and steaming mugs of mulled cider on every autumn Sunday while her and Fleur were growing up. Picca didn't serve it for her family, she didn't let her boys have that much sugar and she assumed Charles only partook to irritate her. Picca served it for their guests, though only a few had ventured out their way today. Their home and livelihood, the D'Avalon Winery, sat on the Canandaigua Wine Trail, and they tended to lose customers earlier in the season than the wineries on the neighboring lakes of Seneca, Cayuga, and Keuka. A fact that Fleur mentioned every autumn.

Picca looked Charles right in the eye and put her arm on his, feeling, like always, that a camera should be following. Her cream blouse looked like the most delicate frosting on top of his deep blue shirt. She whispered to him with a satisfied smile, or what she assumed one would look like, "I'm never disappointed, Charles."

He smiled back, and the anxiety that had caused him to

interfere with the guests' snacks and to underplay the importance of the Christmas card seemed to fade out of him. Once again he was her primary concern, the order now reestablished. Her concerns had taken their place among the trees on the side, whipping by in the distant landscape.

"So, my prince, we can take the picture tomorrow night? It will be great for our brand. I'll pick out the clothes for you and the boys and you can set up the camera in the bedroom and take Maverick for a long walk to tucker him out."

"Affirmative, Captain." Charles, his attention now on the newspaper in his hand, tipped an invisible hat. They'd been sailing once, on their honeymoon. The only time she'd been to Cape Cod, though she often referenced it to customers.

"When we're on the island—that's Martha's Vineyard if you didn't know—we drink unwooded Chardonnays. Perfect with seafood."

"Oh, in Martha's Vineyard we always go to Giordana's. The lobster bisque is to die for."

"Bill and Pat—they run our favorite B&B on the island—Martha's Vineyard, I'm sorry I just always call it the island—are just the best. Tell them the D'Avalons said hello if you see them."

Now that the plan was set, Picca finally let herself get excited for the Christmas card. The idea had come to her quite suddenly just a day before, and the message couldn't have been clearer.

❄

She had been moving the Halloween decorations from the basement up to the lounge, where she would inspect and clean them before putting them on display. The week of Halloween was one of their biggest of the year, despite overall business declining in the autumn. Picca liked to pull out all the stops: pumpkins, cornucopias, gothic candelabras and moody lighting. Classy but evocative.

Searching by lantern light through the basement of their creaky old house, the D'Avalon family home for more than a century, had been like something in a scary movie, the kind she'd loved as a teenager and still snuck as a guilty pleasure if the children and Charles were asleep. She'd tuck her feet under her on their couch and Maverick would snuggle up next to her. Charles' snores would send a slight rumble through the room as he slept in his chair and Picca would put something dark and spooky on the television, sipping a glass of 2005 Bordeaux as someone was inevitably stabbed or strangled.

On her third trip down to the basement, Picca stopped and placed the lantern on Charles' father's old Shaker desk, a sturdy, bland thing that she'd made Charles move down from the study because it didn't match her walnut Montigny bookshelves. She'd rarely even looked at the thing in all of her years in the house, but something was different this time.

Picca wondered if it was the lantern light, or maybe another year of dust, but the desk looked more textured and alive than it ever had before.

The desk itself was rather plain, with a wide work surface and a hefty hutch. The hutch had four letter slots in the center, and these were sandwiched by two small drawers on each side. Picca had never even thought about whether they'd cleaned out the drawers in the hutch before they moved it down to the basement, but the question sprang into her mind and she pulled on the handle of the right bottom drawer. It pulled out about a half an inch but then caught.

It dawned on Picca that she should sell the desk. Shaker furniture was selling for insanely large prices, particularly for such boring designs, and she rarely even thought about the desk. If she were to sell it, though, it would first need all of its drawers to open smoothly. Picca held the lantern up and studied the drawer before grabbing the small metal handle again and wiggled it. After several seconds of rigorous wiggling the drawer popped out. It was empty, but Picca held the lantern up to the empty slot she'd pulled the drawer from, hoping to see what had been obstructing the drawer's path.

It was an envelope. Picca pulled it out carefully, though a trail of dusty cobwebs lurched out with it, as if time were reluctant to give it up. The envelope said nothing on the outside, though on the back was a beautiful, blood red, unbroken wax seal in the shape of a burning plant. At first, Picca thought that it was a Biblical reference, but the long twisty trunk that divided the seal made it obvious that this was a burning tree, not a burning bush.

The top of the envelope had been cut open. Picca delicately reached in and tugged the papers inside, pulling out four individual somethings. She held each by the lantern, feeling like quite the sleuth. The first was a photograph of their home, the D'Avalon estate. It was an old black and white photograph and it must have been taken before the house came into the D'Avalon family, so over a hundred years ago. In the picture, a group of women, at least thirty of them, stood in front of the house. They were all dressed in drab clothing, black and gray and covering every inch of skin. On the bottom of the photo, written out unevenly by what looked to be individual stencils, was "Canandaigua Lake."

The next photograph was of a woman from the shoulders up. It was so old-fashioned that Picca could not tell if it was a photograph or an intricate drawing, but the subject was a proud-faced older woman. The only thing that identified her as a woman was the veil on her head, a light, delicate sort of thing resembling the caps Amish women still wore today. At the bottom, in the same unaligned stenciling, was the name "Mother Ann" and below it, a phrase in quotations: "the wonderful and almost incredible openings of light and truth . . ."

79

The third item was a small, intricate painting, the same size as the photographs but filled with color and minute detail. It was a tree, the trunk of which—just like the one on the wax seal—served to symmetrically divide the tree in two. From each side of the tree burst long branches, shooting out and down towards the ground and then back up again, making the image both one of a tree and one of a cycle of life. The tree was adorned with bright, green, five-pointed leaves and large orange orbs that could have been fruit or orbs of light.

The final thing in the envelope was a postcard. It was an image of four people asleep in a bed. Given that they seemed to have been in this house, it could have even been her and Charles' bedroom. The bed contained two women, one on each edge, and two babies in the middle. The sight of two women sharing a bed hit her unexpectedly, unearthing long-forgotten urges.

She pushed those urges away, returning her attention to the photograph.

The white covers were pulled up to their chests, leaving the women's arms dangling down, two on either side of the babies. Both women wore black lace and it stood out starkly against the white sheets, making it appear that some dark creature caged in the babies.

The babies were mostly covered, their little capped heads being the only exposed part of them. All four bedmates had

had closed eyes and the effect was startling. At first, Picca worried that they might be dead. She'd heard of people keeping records of their dead with photographs taken of the funeral bed. But the bottom of this postcard said "Merry Christmas, 1905" in what appeared to be professional stenciling, not the uneven kind from the photographs.

It was disarming, almost disturbing, and to Picca, entirely unique. What an interesting Christmas greeting. A photograph of peace and tranquility, one that portrayed vulnerability and unity and evoked the most splendid of holiday emotion—of being cozy and asleep in your warm bed.

Picca decided then and there what the D'Avalon Christmas card would be. A night-time photograph of the whole family. An embellished peak behind the curtain into their lives. A glimpse at the D'Avalon lifestyle, the D'Avalon brand.

Once she had cleared the idea with Charles, she needed to get set up for it. New sheets and outfits. Maverick would need to be groomed. But despite her full to do list, Picca couldn't stop thinking about the things she'd found in that envelope. She knew that there had been several spiritual communities in this corner of New York, most significantly the Seneca people for many years and then the Shakers. She sat down at her computer just to take a quick look. The first thing she looked for was "Mother Ann." At first, the sheer amount of nonsense that she'd found was overwhelming. After some skimming and digging, however, Picca was able to start sniffing out the whiffs of truth in the heaps of insane blather she found online. Mother Ann referred to Mother Ann Lee, who had been a leader of the Shakers in the 1700s and was considered by many of them to be the second coming of Jesus Christ.

The Shakers were remembered, at least locally, as a peaceful group. However, the truth of the matter seemed to be much more complicated than that. There were large schisms in the Shaker community. Much of it revolved around the equal footing of men and women. In Shaker communities, women were seen as equal to men, at least at an institutional and spiritual level. However, as Picca knew well, even the most enlightened of men could be pigs. There was also a great deal of back and forth over celibacy and sobriety, two of the primary elements of Shakerism.

Picca wondered whose brilliant idea it had been to isolate entire communities of people, give them all equal say, and prevent them from making love or drinking? What had they thought would happen?

So, while peace, celibacy, and gender equality were all things that the Shakers are remembered for, Picca found that the Shakers struggled mightily over them.

However, even beyond those controversies was the most divisive period of Shaker history, which was called the Era of Manifestations, and this is where Mother Ann Lee really came into play even though she had been dead for quite some time. This was the period of time where the Shaker faith reached its peak and subsequently began to crumble.

After her death in the late 1700s, Mother Ann's visions became famous in Shaker communities, and as word spread, many young Shaker women began to experience visions. They would be suddenly compelled to dance and cry out for hours on end. They would close their eyes and paint pictures of trees and light and fruit while singing. Picca immediately thought of the painting of the tree she'd found in the desk.

Mother Ann had proclaimed that "the wonderful and almost incredible openings of light and truth pertaining to this and the external spiritual world, and which address themselves almost exclusively to the external man, by sensuous facts and physical demonstrations, and which, in former times and other ages, were suppressed and condemned, as the effect of unlawful communings with the powers of darkness, are now being received with joy and gladness by thousands of persons, as proof of a telegraphic communication established between the two worlds."

Mother Ann, and as a result, the majority of Shakers, believed that she had found the secret to opening communication between humans and the spirit world. However, it was only young women who received these visions, or "manifestations."

Shaker men, particularly older ones, became disenchanted with these visions and particularly the deification of Mother Ann Lee following her death. Many Shakers, particularly women, thought of Mother Ann as God in female form, a second coming of Jesus. A basic principle of Shakerism was that God was both male *and* female. Threatened, the Shaker church banned any mention of visions or manifestations and began enforcing even stricter rules involving sobriety and chastity and even food and clothing. When issuing these new rules, the Shaker leaders mentioned being embarrassed by the "emotional excesses and mystical expressions of this period." Picca laughed when she read this. Even back then men were uncomfortable with women expressing emotion.

As she learned all of this, pieces began to fall in place in Picca's mind. But she still couldn't figure out how it all applied to their home. Why had there been a picture of all of those women at the D'Avalon Estate? She did find a Shaker community, Groveland, long dormant, about thirty miles down the road from them.

Then, Picca thought to research the D'Avalons. What she found, on a free trial on *Ancestry*.com, was that a French Canadian trader named Guy D'Avalon had bought the property

from an entity called *The Sisters of the Blazing Tree*. In looking into them, Picca found some more answers. After the
Shakers banned visions in the mid-1800s, many left the
church and started their own communities. One such community was made up of young women who experienced
visions and who produced art depicting what they had seen
in their visions. They farmed the land to live and acted as a
shelter for women on the run, welcoming anyone into their
community as long as they would respect their customs and
help out on the farm. They called themselves the Sisters of
the Blazing Tree. Their community had sat right on Canandaigua Lake, in a house gifted to them by the bachelor son of
long dead Shakers. Shakers were given the choice, at age
twenty-one, to decide whether to leave the faith—and thus
their families—forever, or to stay. The problem with that
choice is that staying with the Shakers meant celibacy, not a
choice any twenty-one year old would choose. Picca wondered if this man who gave the Sisters his home was trying to
make amends with his long dead parents, to apologize for
leaving them. A feeling Picca could understand all too well.

Over the years, while the Sisters of the Blazing Tree grew
and flourished, the Groveland Shakers diminished. Their
adherence to celibacy and simplicity failed to attract new
members. Picca found quite a few mentions of fighting between the Sisters of the Blazing Tree and the Groveland

Shakers. In the early 1900s, the Sisters of the Blazing Tree had grown so large that they sold the farm and moved to a larger community in Vermont. Their settlement there eventually became an artist colony, open to all, and remained to this day, though Picca found no mention of visions or manifestations on their website.

The card felt even more important now. Their home had been a place of art and worship, a reprieve from the cold, stark world of men. That deserved to be celebrated, and how better, even if only just for herself, to do so with a holiday homage?

Picca gave one last thought to Mother Ann Lee before heading out to get ready for the picture. Worshipped as God during life and after death, a protector of women and leader of men. Picca felt close to her, an affinity for her, an *attraction* to her, though they were separated by over two hundred years.

❄

Picca had assembled their twins, Bobby and Jack, their panting Samoyed, Maverick, and Charles in the master suite. Everything was in order: the twins and Maverick were exhausted and all five of them looked great. Picca had taken the twins shopping in Geneva and sugared them up with Orange Juliuses and Dairy Queen Blizzards, things she normally would have not allowed, and now they were crashing. Charles had hiked Maverick down in High Tor.

Picca had made the bed in five hundred count Charter Club Damask sheets. They were a beautiful red, so deep that they were almost Burgundy. Maverick was wearing his Christmas collar, which was Tiffany blue, as were the boys' pajamas, the dusty color complimenting their pale gold hair. She wore a night set in a Scotland Road shade of white, from Nordstrom, and cinched the belt around her waist to accentuate her figure. She had Charles wear a modest Calvin Klein tank and pajama bottom combination. Despite his doughnut thievery, he had kept a muscular physique, particularly his toned biceps, one of the things that Picca had first noticed about him when then had met at a Cornell alumni dinner all of those years ago. The perfect trophy.

"Okay team, here's the plan!" Charles was fiddling with the camera and the twins were about to keel over.

"We're having a family slumber party. Your father is going to set up the camera to take a picture every hour. The bed is more than big enough for the five of us to sleep. Try to sleep on your sides. Boys, try to face the same direction. We'll have Maverick lie across the bottom of the bed. And then the picture will be of all of us, snuggled together, just like *The Night Before Christmas*."

"That sounds really weird, Mom," was Jack's comment.

Picca was not hurt. She'd known it would seem a little strange to them, and she'd purposely not told them anything about the card she'd found in the basement. She could see the card in her mind's eye. She could seem them all sleeping in their bed with its mahogany headboard, carved with images of grapes, which had seemed a bit overboard when she'd bought it but now felt like genius. She would be wrapped in one of her husband's strong arms, her beautiful babies sleeping peacefully next to her, their perfectly groomed dog warming their feet. Inside the card, she would put a verse from *The Night Before Christmas* with a few slight changes:

> *'Twas the night before Christmas, when all through
>   the house
> Not a creature was stirring, not even a mouse;
> The stockings were hung by the chimney with care,
> In hopes that St. Nicholas soon would be there;
> The D'Avalons were nestled all snug in their beds,
> While visions of Bordeaux grapes danced in
>   their heads.*
>
> ## Happy Holidays from D'Avalon Winery*
>
> *This card can be redeemed on site
> for a free bottle of our Cape Concord Dessert Wine*

The card would remain on refrigerators for months, until the recipients decided to come wine tasting in the spring or summer, long after Fleur's card was thrown in the garbage.

"I'll make French toast for breakfast if you sleep here, lovelings."

They stopped protesting and hopped into the bed. Charles set the camera and then settled in. He patted the bed beside him indicating her spot while smiling. For the first time in a long while, she was excited to get into bed with him. He was getting into the spirit and the result she had imagined, the Christmas card, was within reach. She turned off the overhead light, leaving only electric candles. She'd considered real candles but couldn't justify the risk of burning them all to death, even if it were for the perfect Christmas card.

Picca tried to clear her mind. She didn't want to rustle, knowing that she had to keep her head angled just so to avoid having a double chin in the photo. She imagined fields of grapes and falling snow and sugar maples rustling in the wind. After some time, still wide-awake, she heard the distinctive *click!* of the camera. She opened an eye and saw Charles was asleep, a slight smile on his face. She wondered what, or who, he was dreaming about.

She gingerly craned her neck trying to glimpse the boys. They were also sleeping deeply, on their sides just as she'd told them, and Bobby's hand was adorably reaching up and lightly mussing Jack's hair. *Perfect!*

Once again she tried to imagine peaceful pastures, quiet forests, and gentle landscapes in order to induce sleep. Her mind led her to an image of the forest, unseasonably green and verdant. She didn't know how she knew, but she knew that in her mind's eye this forest was in autumn, but that it had somehow resisted death. As her focus narrowed, she saw individual trees. One tree in particular struck her. It was symmetrical, perfectly symmetrical. Picca knew that almost nothing in nature was truly symmetrical, truly perfect, re-gardless of how much she wished it so. But this tree was. The tree was a nest of five-pointed leaves, like sugar maple leaves but radiating light from beneath their green veneer. As she watched, the tree rose from the dirt, lifting its roots upward like a lady in long dress preparing to dance. It's sharp move-ments, graceful but jagged, made the tree insect-like, and as it rose from the dirt it inspired its sister trees to also rise. They all rose up, and while Picca was aware of the others her mind's eye was pinned to this one symmetrical tree, which began to dance. Its branches were pitching inward from its sides and then shooting back out from its base, as if it were consuming and birthing itself in perpetuity. It was strange and alien yet also completely familiar.

Quite suddenly, Picca felt as if she weren't only watching the tree, but instead that she herself *was* also a tree. Rather than a feeling of sisterhood, however, it was an erotic feeling, an expression of feminine force and beauty. She reveled in it and she felt burst after burst of stimuli as her own roots mingled in the ground with those of this other tree.

As suddenly as her meditation had turned into feverish dream Pica was ejected from the dream, opening her eyes and gasping awake. Light shone through the windows and she was alone in the bed. She usually woke clear-minded, but now the sensation was extreme; she was hyper-aware. She couldn't believe that she had even been asleep, so vivid was her dream. And there were no gaps in her memory: her attempts to sleep had transitioned directly into the dream and now to morning. Where had the time gone?

Picca rose and padded out to the kitchen, where she found Charles sitting at the counter with the paper, a steaming cup of coffee in front of him. After what she'd seen in her dream, what she'd *felt*, Charles looked irrevocably boring, blunt and hard and hazy.

"Hey sleepyhead," he said. "I can't remember the last time you slept in. Our honeymoon?"

"Me neither," Picca responded, bewildered. She was on edge, the bright light streaming through the window dim in comparison to the dream, which she still could see vividly in her mind.

"Do you want the good news or the bad news?" Charles asked.

Picca heard him, but it didn't register. She'd been looking forward to something but all she could think about was the symmetrical tree, crawling up from the earth and dancing.

"Earth to Picca. Darling, are you listening? Maybe you should go back to bed." Picca could hear the concern in Charles' voice and, with some difficulty, directed her attention to him.

"Sorry," she said. "I must still be a bit sleepy." Which wasn't true, but she felt compelled to keep the dream to herself. It felt very personal, though she didn't know why.

"I said there is good news and bad news."

Picca poured herself a cup of coffee. "Where are the boys?" she asked.

"They're at hockey. Are you listening to me?"

Picca looked him in the eyes, amber like autumn leaves. She searched his face for annoyance, eager to lash out something, to use some of her crackling nervous energy. She told herself, as always, to remain calm.

"Yes, darling. What's all of this bad news?"

"Most of the pictures didn't work out."

For a moment she couldn't think of what pictures he could be speaking about. Then she remembered the missing camera, then the reason they'd all been in bed together. The Christmas card. How had she let it slip her mind?

"Oh no! What's the problem?"

"It's you."

Picca grabbed the counter. Charles was at her side in seconds, hand on her elbow.

"It's not that you don't look stunning darling, it's just the camera did something to you. There's a smudge over you in nearly all of the pictures."

She wanted to smack him, but remembered to play her part.

"Oh no!" she cried. "What kind of smudge?"

Charles grabbed the camera off of the counter and pulled it up so they could both look at the pictures on the digital screen.

Her first thought was that yes, this picture, this idea, was perfect. They were beautiful. Relaxed, peaceful. The perfect family. If it were not for the hazy white smudge that covered most of her body. The smudge was worst right down the middle of the bed, mixing the white from Picca's night set and the red of the bed with a milky pink fuzziness. It reminded Picca of television static. Looking closer, Picca saw that the smudge extended beyond the middle of the bed. Three symmetrical lines of static extended from each side of the center, making six long additional smudges. In its whole, it looked to Picca like a hazy cage superimposed over her.

Charles pressed a button on the camera and it moved to the next picture. This one was nearly identical except that

Bobby had turned over and had his hand stretched across Jack's head, ruffling his hair. Adorable, Picca thought. But the smudge was even harder to ignore in this one. It had moved to the left, its center now right side, though the lines extended fully across both sides of the bed.

Charles pointed to the screen. "It's not a smudge on the lens, because it moves a little in every picture."

Picca watched as he scrolled through. Her heart sank as the smudge grew more noticeable in each picture.

"Didn't you say you had good news?" Picca asked.

Charles nodded and kept clicking. The smudge moved a little bit in every one, almost like it too was shifting in its sleep. In the second to last photo, the smudge wasn't on Picca. It was off the side of the bed, beyond Charles. It wasn't the best of the photos. Charles' mouth was open slightly and Maverick's lip had stuck in his teeth, making it look as if he were growling.

"Do you think we can use this one, *mi amour*?" she asked.

"Yep. I'll just crop it. And I can fix up some little things in Photoshop."

"I wonder what caused the smudge. Does it disappear after this?"

"No, look at the next one."

In the final picture, taken at 6:30 in the morning, the smudge was its most concentrated. The center of the smudge and its accompanying lines were thicker in this picture, but they also appeared to Picca to be less straight lines and more segmented. She took a closer look at it.

There was nothing human about it. But Picca couldn't help but think of Mother Ann Lee. Picca knew it was because she had read so much about her yesterday. Obviously it had caused her to have weird dreams about the tree, and Mother Ann must still be sitting in her subconscious. Her imagination told her there was more to it, that she was missing something big here. If there was anything Picca was good at, it was cutting out distraction. She told Charles to go back to the previous picture.

It was perfect. "Lover, can you get this cropped and onto the computer? I can't wait to have the card made."

Charles smiled at her. "Of course. Look at you, looking at the bright side."

A seed had been planted. For days and then weeks, Picca pushed it way. She was thrilled with the Christmas card. When the boxes came from the printer's she ripped one open and marveled at how well the idea had been executed. As she stared at their sleeping faces, however, she felt as if the picture were missing something. The smudge, she thought, before telling herself to snap out of it.

They sent the card out on Thanksgiving, certain that it would arrive well before Christmas. Fleur's card, which arrived on December 1st, was the image of a blown glass hanging sculpture meant to evoke grapes. It looked cold and brittle compared to their warm family card. Picca thought perhaps she'd get a snide phone call of some sort once Fleur received their card, but when they didn't she took even more delight. Picca was sure Fleur was at home fuming, thinking of what she could possibly do to undermine Picca at Christmas dinner.

Picca returned to the basement for Christmas decorations in early December and once again placed her lantern on the old Shaker desk. Charles had put the Halloween decorations away, as usual, so this was her first time back since discovering the pictures several months before. She carefully pulled the envelope out from beneath the lower right hand drawer, where she'd returned it after her first encounter with the images. She slid them out of the envelope one by one and looked at them. When she saw Mother Ann's face, she felt warm affection. She traced her hand across it. The tree, that tree of her dreams, was more vivid in her mind's eye now than it had been when she saw it last. She looked at all of the faces of the Sisters of the Blazing Tree standing in their yard, in *her* yard, and felt a responsibility to them. And finally, she looked at those sleeping women and their sleeping babies. She pulled a photo out of the pocket of her beige romper she'd gotten from Talbott's a few days prior. It was a picture of her family sleeping, peaceful in their beds. Her guardian angel, as she'd come to think of her, Mother Ann, floating above her, appearing in the photo as an incredible opening of light and truth, hanging right above her. She placed that photo with the one of the women, slid all of the pictures back into the envelope, and returned it to the drawer.

Picca had always felt more special than where she was from. *Whom* she was from. Now, she knew she was special. She knew that every decision she'd made, everything she had questioned, made perfect sense. If she hadn't let Fleur buy her out of her half of her parents' beloved farm, if she hadn't married Charles because she liked him a little and liked his family's property a lot, if she had never come to the D'Avalon farm and invested her inheritance and become trapped here, she never would have discovered her gift. The gift given to her by Mother Ann Lee and the Sisters of the Blazing Tree.

She grabbed a box of silver bulbs for the tree she'd put in the formal dining room. Usually they put a smaller blue spruce in there to compliment the big tree they'd put in the living room, but this year she found a prematurely fallen young sugar maple, unearthed by a storm and put it in a pot in the corner. She covered it with silver and watered it. Though it appeared dead, soon an unseen force would rise through its veins and return life to its branches.

As Picca considered this, the image of the tree once again invaded her mind, and she felt a presence envelope her. Its warm breath brushed her neck and caused her to flush. She, too, felt the life returning to her, pouring in through an incredible opening of light.

MOMBASA VENGEANCE

The tale of my journey to Mombasa requires little prelude. The coward Ezekial Greyhorn, a merchant and a scoundrel, had murdered my wife, Cornelia, and I intended to kill him for it. Unfortunately for Greyhorn, I was a very wealthy man, and the death of my wife made me wealthier still. As the fourth son of a baroness and an earl, I inherited no title but considerable means; my wife's lineage, on the other hand, was superior to my own, being the third child of a countess and a viscount. She and I lived in a lovely white-stuccoed house on the east terrace of Belgrave Square in Belgravia, a district in London that had once been owned in its entirety by my wife's great-grandfather Richard Grosvenor, 2nd Marquess of Westminster.

Greyhorn had murdered his own wife as well as mine with poison (a craven's implement), a fact I would not have discovered had he not told me so in a letter. By the time I received it, Greyhorn was long gone, his home in Clapham sold. However, being a merchant, Greyhorn relied on business relationships, and it didn't take me long to find that he'd left a forwarding address with Burroughs Wellcome & Co, a pharmaceutical supplier in Wandsworth. According to their impressionable young secretary—a sturdy young man with a strong chin and a full, inviting mouth—Greyhorn had seen the light of the Lord and left to establish an outpost for the import of medical supplies to aid missionaries in British East Africa. I was certain this had less to do with Greyhorn's yearning for God's grace and more to do with the deep pockets of the Imperial British East Africa Company, which was throwing money in every direction in order to justify their expensive and deadly railway, which linked the port city of Mombasa to Nairobi in the northwest and then westward still to Kisumu on the eastern shore of Lake Victoria.

The Mombasa address that Greyhorn had left with Burroughs Wellcome was that of an inn called The Bender's Arms.

At first I was going to send my son Charlie off to boarding school while I traveled in Africa. The logical part of my brain told me this was the right decision. However, as my inability to avoid succumbing to my unique proclivities could attest, the logical part of my brain was rarely in control. Emotion told me to bring Charlie along, to imbue his teenage years with adventure that my own had lacked. Further, I came to the conclusion that I would not be returning to England. If all went according to plan, Charlie would return to London with sun-kissed skin, a large inheritance (perhaps a title if a few aunts and uncles died childless), and memories of his father's bravery—and the satisfaction of knowing that he had played a part in avenging his beloved mother.

That's how Charlie and I found ourselves on a cool morning in April of 1910 boarding the *S.S. Berwick Castle* on the famous Union-Castle Line, headed south to Mombasa directly from Southampton. The *Berwick* was a majestic ship, its base vibrant lavender with a line of bright red barely visible below it, like lips kissing the sea. Above the base the ship was pristine white, like a Greek temple perched atop Jason's Argo. It had a single, black-tipped funnel poking out the top, and the smoke was already pouring out.

"Jasper and Charles Beck. First class." I said to the first Union-Castle representative we happened upon, a polished but vacant-eyed fellow. He snapped to attention and motioned for a porter, who led us straight from our carriage to a steep gangplank that took us up to the first-class deck, bypassing both the tourist class passengers and the stevedores loading parcels and mail crates onto the ship. As our porter, Bartholomew ("call me Bart"), led us along the polished deck, we passed the crew being inspected by several stern-looking officers. This theatrical display was obviously for the benefit of higher-paying passengers, and I tipped my hat at the blank-faced crew members as we passed, pleased to note more than a few handsome faces.

Charlie scurried along by my side, simultaneously trying to take in the sights and keep up with Bart and me. I'd dressed him in his own little sailor suit: a white canvas set with blue tapes sewn on to mimic a naval uniform. His mother had bought it for him the year before and I'd had my tailor update it for the journey. At ten, he was almost too old for it, but Charlie had a keen sense of whimsy and I wanted him to feel as light-hearted as possible, if only to offset my bloody intent.

Bart informed us that there were forty first-class state-rooms and one hundred tourist class cabins, accounting for a total of three hundred and one passengers. We would take our meals in the first-class dining room and could entertain ourselves in the first-class gymnasium, smoking room, sa-loon, or reading room, while activities like cricket, shuffleboard, and tug-of-war would take place on the main deck, which could be accessed by descending one of the staircases in the foyer.

Charlie was thrilled by the idea of on-deck games while I was thrilled with by the idea of sitting in the saloon and drinking myself numb. When we reached our stateroom, number twenty-two, Bart leaned in and whispered that there was also a governess on board should I need any "private time." I looked down at Charlie, with his pink cheeks and the shy expression he'd worn like a shroud ever since his mother had been taken from us, and I couldn't imagine sending him away for even a second. That said, we'd not yet spent twenty days on the water together, so I kept the governess in mind.

The stateroom itself was beautifully outfitted. The sitting room had a peridot carpet and a small circular window with curtains in a deeper hue of green. There were separate bedrooms for the two of us, each with a sizable bed, mirror, and closet. All of the furniture was made of fine dark wood and upholstered in soft fabric.

And there was a water closet. How such a thing was possible on a ship was beyond me, and I didn't want to ask Bart for specifics for fear he'd say something unseemly about sewage and ruin my appetite. There was a sink and a small bathtub, both with shining brass fixtures. Bart told me to ring the bell by our door if we needed hot water—or anything else—brought in. Otherwise, we could use the first class baths by the gymnasium or visit the barber.

Charlie began jumping on his bed and I slipped the porter some coins. Before he left, he handed me a beautifully handwritten menu on pale green paper. Dinner would be a choice of Supreme of Fresh Haddock Cardinal with Potage Longchamps or Epigrammes of Lamb Villeroi with Cauliflower Polonaise. Obviously the chef was French.

"Dinner is at eight o'clock, Sir Beck" he said with a smile. "Your place settings will be labeled by name, but your chairs also correspond to your room number, if you should forget your spectacles."

I absently reached up and adjusted my glasses, surprised that Bart had mentioned them.

"Oh these? They're just for fashion," I lied. "Not that it's any of your business."

Bart flushed red and apologized profusely, which in turn made me feel a bit wretched, though he was entirely at fault. The glasses were a sensitivity; they were new and usually bothered me a great deal, but I'd forgotten them for a few moments. Now I felt old again, despite being barely thirty. A year ago I'd been in my twenties, married, with perfectly functioning faculties. Now I was a widower in his thirties with failing eyesight. Time was cruel.

"May I suggest, sir, drinks in the saloon beforehand?" Bart tried, eager to change the subject. "The windows will afford a beautiful view of the sunset."

I thanked Bart and he departed, leaving Charlie and me alone in the stateroom. The air was a bit stale, so I opened the window, letting the fresh Southampton breeze flow in. The trip would only get warmer.

Someone would be along with our luggage soon, though I didn't yet require it. I had dressed formally in order to board the ship, so my top hat, white-collared shirt, black frock coat with a deep blue waistcoat beneath (to bring out my eyes), and tightly tailored trousers would be suitable for dinner. My personal style was a bit old-fashioned, more in tune with my father's generation, but I preferred a tighter fit and brighter colors than the baggy, black-on-black ensembles that were currently the fashion among the upper crust.

Charlie's sailor suit would be perfect for dinner, certain to charm our tablemates. Like his mother before him, Charlie reveled in attention, and God had gifted him with his mother's blond curls and his father's bright blue eyes, so people did just that.

I was grateful that I'd decided against bringing a valet along. Though Charlie and I were both used to assistance in dressing, bathing, and disrobing, we were perfectly able to do so on our own, and it would diminish our adventure if we were to stop every few minutes to have some clucking servant readjust our handkerchiefs. In addition, a valet would make a fuss over us, insisting we change for dinner. Charlie would have to wash behind his ears and change into a fresh combination while I'd have to oil my hair, reapply cologne, and change into freshly shined shoes. We were going it on our own now, like the cowboys in America, and we'd have to learn to take care of ourselves.

A loud horn sounded through the air just as I sat down on

Charlie's bed next to him to show him the dinner menu. It sounded like some kind of mythic goose, wild and free. I couldn't yet feel the ship move but I could see the landscape slowly shift outside the stateroom's small window.

"We're going to Africa!" Charlie exclaimed, jumping to his feet on the bed again.

I looked at Charlie but my mind's eye was on Ezekial Greyhorn, on his blood coating my fingers as the life bled out of him.

"Yes we are," I said, smiling.

Our twenty days on the *S.S. Berwick Castle* were much like our days in Belgravia, except that Charlie didn't have to attend lessons and I didn't have to keep my appearance nearly as polished. Normally I went to the barber once a week for a trim, and my valet kept my sideburns immaculate. But aboard the *Berwick* I let my hair grow, my copper-brown curls now reaching my ears. I still went for shaves, however. A clean shave and tight pants were strong hints that one was a homosexual, and since other hints were too dangerous, I chose to advertise as subtlety as I could.

The air had indeed gotten hotter and hotter as we'd gone south, going from pleasant warmth in the Mediterranean to hot and muggy in the Suez Canal and Red Sea, to blistering and scorching as we rounded the Horn of Africa and approached Mombasa. Mombasa is almost exactly on the Equator, so there would be no relief: only more heat, more blinding sun.

By day nineteen, Charlie and I were spending most of our days sprawled on our separate beds in our underwear. Poor Charlie wore combinations and thus was covered from shoulder to thigh, and I worried the poor boy would boil before we reached Mombasa.

Meals were an uncomfortable affair. Our tablemates, a friendly Omani couple, were not only used to hot weather in their home country, but also traveled regularly to Mombasa and Zanzibar for their family business and as such were quite used to the heat. Charlie and I, on the other hand, looked horribly unkempt in comparison, our faces flushed by the omnipresent heat and our hair curled by the humidity.

When we finally landed in Mombasa on day twenty, I wondered how I planned on killing Ezekial Greyhorn if I couldn't walk ten feet without feeling faint. Before we left the ship, Bart appeared to help us repack our things. While he busied himself with Charlie's bedroom, in which Charlie had built a fort by tying his dress shirts from his bedposts to the lamps in the corners of his room, I withdrew my pistol, a small Browning, from my luggage. I slipped it into my pants, right at the small of my back, and adjusted my waistcoat over it, hopeful that I thus concealed it without making my back and hindquarters look deformed.

Charlie was busy peering out our window as we approached Kilindini Harbor. I walked up behind him and placed my hands on his shoulders. I'd allowed him to choose his own outfit for arrival and he'd chose his American suit, a miniature cowboy outfit, complete with a wide-brimmed hat and brown, sharp-tipped leather boots. As I held his small shoulders and watched the island that Mombasa sat upon approach I suddenly felt breathless. We might meet Ezekial Greyhorn within minutes of landing on those shores. And I meant to murder him. How could I kill a man in front of the eyes of my own child?

I knew that I had to. Charlie would soon be old enough to notice how different his father was. He'd notice how carefully I shaved my face, how delicately I moved my fingers. He'd notice my lack of interest in the ladies we passed in the street, and he'd see my cheeks flush when I stopped and spoke to a handsome gentlemen.

But if Charlie saw me avenge his mother (who, if there were any silver lining to her death, it was that she had died before Charlie noticed *her* eccentricities), then he would remember that act and that alone. He would recall me as if I were a hero of ancient myth, driven by righteous vengeance and masculine retribution. I'd send him back to England with his pockets overflowing, and a heavy but proud heart.

We exited the ship with several strapping young men following us with our luggage, and a Union-Castle representative organized a carriage for us into town from Kilindini Harbor.

As we left the port and drove into Mombasa, I was surprised by its eclectic yet predominantly European appearance. The city had been founded hundreds of years before and for that reason I had assumed it would be African through and through, which in my mind meant constructions of wood, mud, brightly colored fabric, and rough animal hides.

Instead, Mombasa looked like the result of an allied effort among Portugal, England, and Arabia. Most of the newer buildings were white stucco, wood, or brick, and featured gables and Baroque windows, nearly a Queen Anne style except with lower roofs. The older buildings resembled Portuguese forts, lower to the ground with a pinkish-orange hue and blocky construction. Finally, there was an abundance of mosques and other stone buildings with large overhangs and patterns carved into or painted on their exteriors.

The people in the streets were even more diverse than the architecture. Watching and explaining them to Charlie took my mind off of the pistol pressing sharply into my back and the twisting of my stomach at the thought of sinking a righteous bullet into Greyhorn's duplicitous skull.

The residents of Mombasa varied wildly, from black Africans of both sexes in light one-shouldered robes, to Arabians in white clothing and extravagant headwear, the men in bright red fezzes and the ladies in *jalibib*. Most abundant, however, were Englishmen. There were a few ladies, but mostly the streets were filled with ambling men in black suits more in the current style than my own, with baggy trousers, no waistcoats, and loose-fitting coats. Several wore smocks, which was probably a smart alternative with respect to the heat but made those wearing them look like coalminers. And a very small number, likely tourists on hunting holidays, wore white leisure suits, looking like big, cotton-swathed infants.

We arrived in front of the Bender's Arms at half past four in the afternoon. The heat was fading just a bit, transitioning from deadly to unbearable, and I longed for a pint of ale and some shade. I kept reaching back unconsciously to rub the pistol in the small of my back and then sharply yanking my hand away when I realized what I was doing. Charlie hopped out of the carriage ahead of me. I threw the driver some coins and asked him to please wait a few minutes while we organized our rooms.

"When will we see a lion, Daddy?" Charlie asked, his blond brows knitted together in quite a serious expression.

"Soon, my boy, though hopefully not too soon!" I said.

"I want to see one now, though," he whined desperately. The heat was making him irritable and I decided to get both of us beer—provided we didn't run into Greyhorn as soon as we entered the inn, in which case things would play out a bit differently.

The Bender's Arms was a lovely three-story building made out of deep brown wood. It had three gables, each ornamented with a fine lattice of what looked to be bamboo, making it a sort of African gingerbread house. I grabbed Charlie's hand and pulled him inside with me, and we both sighed in relief upon entering the inn's cool ground floor. The entrance was two stories tall, long and wide with a high ceiling. There were staircases to our left and right, leading up to a balcony that ran around three sides of the room's interior. Rooms were visible along the balcony at the top, each clearly marked with a large number carved out of some kind of soft wood. There were six rooms visible and presumably more on the third floor and out back.

The ground floor was filled with tables and chairs, and a large bar took up nearly the entire wall opposite where Charlie and I stood at the entrance. Half of the bar's roughly twenty stools were filled with men of various background, shapes, and sizes, and the diversity was a striking contrast to most of the public houses I frequented in London.

I scanned the room and saw no sign of Ezekial Greyhorn. I'd met him quite a few times, as Cornelia and I had frequented the stall he and his wife had operated in Borough Market. He was a tall, rail-thin man with bright, straw-colored hair and a thin, scraggly beard. He had the spare chessboard teeth of a man who'd survived a hungry childhood, and as a result his cheeks were sunken, making his wide cheekbones look even larger.

I was relieved and disappointed at his absence. One hand still at the pistol at my back, I guided Charlie forward with the other, sitting him down at one of the tables. I put a hand to his cheek. He was much too warm.

"You stay here, my boy, while I get us some drinks. If anyone speaks to you, just scream for me."

I removed his leather jacket and put it on the back of his chair, gave his shoulders a squeeze, and proceeded to the bar.

The barman was hideously ugly. His ruddy face was pockmarked on one side and almost entirely destroyed by a lumpy pink scar on the other. The scar ran from his left ear across to the bridge of his nose and then down the left side of his face to his lips. It pulled the top lip up and bottom lip down, revealing teeth as soft and yellow as honey cake.

The barman eyed me with what appeared to be vigorous dislike, although it was hard to tell on account of his grotesque visage. Behind him, a striking black African in a white collared shirt and tight black trousers was pushing wooden barrels into the bar area from a large black doorway, presumably from the basement.

"I would like—" I started, looking at the barman's pea green good eye.

"We don't cater to pederasty here," he interrupted, his sneer revealing more rotting teeth.

For a moment I was extremely confused. Then I saw his good eye flick over my shoulder. I followed his gaze, spotting the back of Charlie's ringlet-covered head as he sat quietly at the table where I'd left him.

I glared at the barman incredulously.

"I see that your thoughts are as disgusting as your face," I hissed, returning his sneer.

He had the good grace to step back, his cheeks reddening.

"That's my son, you halfwit. And if you expect to win customers by accusing them of abusing the innocent, then I assure you that approach will fail with me. Buying this establishment out from under your plague-bitten arse would be as inconsequential as purchasing a pot of tea, so watch your tone."

He reddened further.

"I'm s-s-s-sorry, sir!" he squealed. He glanced over his shoulder at the African, who had stopped pushing barrels and was regarding us with interest.

"It's just that we have a few ladies upstairs, and we've been getting a disturbing amount of enquiries about young-sters from Englishmen lately—which we *do not* supply! And then I saw you enter with the child, and I thought that was your taste," he whispered abjectly, not meeting my eyes.

That left me feeling rather awful. This man had simply been protecting children from predators, whereas I had feared he'd been making gross assumptions based on my effeminate manner.

"That's fine," I said, clearing my throat. I cautioned a glance around and saw that everyone in the establishment was staring at me with the exception of Charlie, who was staring towards the front door, likely watching pedestrians meander past. Perhaps I should have refrained from so loudly declaring my wealth.

I was certain that Ezekial Greyhorn had been one of the disgusting men pursuing young girls and it emboldened me. I needed no extra motivation to murder him, but it had been delivered nonetheless.

"I'd like to arrange a room. Preferably two connected rooms, but one room with two beds will function just fine."

"Of course, sir. We've got a suite out back—it's half under-ground, so it's nice and cool—and it has a lounge and two bedrooms. And its own outhouse!" he added enthusiastically, as if al fresco elimination were something to be proud of.

"That sounds functional enough," I said. "My carriage is out front. Can you have our luggage brought to our rooms?"

"Of course, sir," he said, finally looking up. Where his face had looked hideous before, it now looked profoundly sad. Endearingly so, like a pitiful French mime.

"And could you have your boy bring a pint of ale and a half pint of *Apfelwein* to our table?" I said, motioning towards the African who had returned to pushing barrels up into the bar.

The barman shook his head and looked over his shoulder, where the African had stopped pushing barrels. He stood up and approached me quickly. He was quite striking. His clothes fit him like bronze fits a statue. I wondered if he spoke English, and why he was approaching me so aggressively. My hand again returned to my back, where I felt the comforting bulge of the pistol.

"I own this establishment, and I'm no one's *boy*," the African declared.

I didn't know if I was more surprised by his revelation or by the fact that he delivered it with a Scottish accent. I was momentarily at a loss for words. Instead, I just stared at the man and his ugly bartender, waiting for inspiration to strike.

"I know you Limeys have trouble with black people doing anything other than serving," he said tersely. "So if this is a problem for you, you know where the door is."

"I don't have any problem at all," I said. And I meant it, although it was a new concept to me. I couldn't recall seeing any black faces at all back home. As a boy my father had read me news of black freedom in America during Abraham Lincoln's presidency, but I'd never really thought about it in Africa. I just assumed that black Africans had their own towns and that colonists had theirs. I could have read something on the subject before our departure, but I'd been too occupied envisioning sweet revenge.

The owner's face softened. He put an arm around the barman's back and said, "James, go and find Victor and have him take their bags to Mary's Suite. I'll pour the drinks," he said, giving the ugly man a pat.

James hustled off and the owner held out his hand to me. "I'm Musa. What brings you to Mombasa, Mister . . . ?"

I wondered if I should correct him and tell him that my title was *Sir*, but I didn't think that would raise his opinion of me.

Instead, I shook his hand and said, "I'm Jasper Beck. And that's my son Charles over there."

His eyes were so dark brown that it was nearly impossible to make out his pupils. He looked me up and down, lingering a bit too long. I felt a flush. He brought his eyes back up to my own and met them deeply, holding a stare. I couldn't look away. His face was kind but also mischievous. Something about his expression warned that at any moment he was going to get one over on me. I wondered if he was having

Victor throw my luggage into the stable or planning on mixing some kind of hallucinogenic African root into my beer.

James returned and took our drinks from Musa and delivered them to the table where Charlie sat. Charlie turned around and looked to me for approval and I nodded and called, "I'll be over in a minute. Drink the *Apfelwein*. Not too fast."

I turned back to Musa and James.

"How much do I owe you?" I asked.

"We'll put it on the bill for your room," Musa said. "How long do you intend to stay?"

"That depends on a couple of things," I said, my mouth suddenly dry. Perhaps I should have had some beer before explaining myself, though surely that wasn't what heroic avengers did, was it?

"Depends on what?" Musa asked.

I was too nervous to answer. He was taller than me by about four inches, and I considered myself tall. His questioning seemed particularly intense when aimed downwards. "What happened to your face?" I asked James. I instantly regretted it. It had simply been the first thing beyond murdering Ezekial Greyhorn that my mind could grasp.

Musa looked surprised, but James smiled a big, ugly smile.

"It was my brother! Stuck to my face. They cut us apart at birth. My mother said it's why I'm such an angel, because the devil took him. He was all shriveled and had pointy little fingers. But I think he was my twin, that he's living on the other side, just as happy as me, waiting to be stuck together again."

I just stared, mouth agape. I'd been expecting a battle story, or perhaps something involving fishing. Still, the revelation loosened me up a bit, and I got to the point.

"This establishment is listed as the address of a man named Ezekial Greyhorn," I said, watching Musa and James for their reactions. Musa's face remained blank, while James' lit up. "Do you know him?"

"Zeke! Yep! In fact, Musa's in—Ow!"

A loud thump had come from somewhere behind the bar and James was now hopping on one foot.

Musa said, "Why do you ask?"

I wondered if I should dissemble. Then, remembering that I was an angel of vengeance—a hero, not a coward—I said, "I intend to kill him."

James mouth dropped open. Musa looked at me like I'd just belched in his face. All around us at the bar, men gasped.

James sputtered, "What do you mean, kill him? Where do you think you are? Texas?"

Musa joined in. "This isn't some lawless American outpost where you can just shoot people! This is Africa! We have *rules!*"

"He killed my wife!" My words came out in a disastrously high timbre.

James turned to some muttering guests further down the bar and produced an obviously fake guffaw. "He's such a jokester, our friend here," James said to them, looking back at Musa nervously.

"Why don't I help you and your son get settled in Mary's Suite?" Musa said, grabbing my arm forcefully over the bar.

"Certainly," I said, looking back to Charlie, who had downed his *Apfelwein* and started on my ale. He'd be asleep in a matter of minutes.

"Follow me," Musa said grimly and pointed towards the door.

I got an already-sleeping Charlie settled in the adjoining bed-room and met Musa in the lounge. He'd brought a bottle of whiskey and two glasses along and set them on a small yellow table in the middle of the dim room. Calling it a suite was a stretch, but it was even cooler than the main building and was clean.

Musa stretched himself out in a chair, his long, lean body looking distractingly inviting. The top two buttons of his shirt were unbuttoned, which seemed entirely inappropriate, but the look did suit him. I removed my frock coat and sat across from him. I'd worn another of my bright blue waistcoats to accentuate my eyes and I found myself wishing I'd applied more cologne before exiting the ship. I comforted myself by remembering that when I'd planned my outfit I'd been intending to murder a merchant, not seduce an innkeeper.

Musa poured us each two fingers and then said, his eyes kind, "Tell me your story."

"It's pretty sordid," I said before knocking back my whole glass.

Musa poured me another and smiled.

"I like sordid," he said.

"Fine then," I said. "But I won't hold back. Be prepared to be scandalized."

He gave me a dark look that made my toes curl. "I look forward to it."

I began.

"Cornelia and I met at one of a series of horrible dances the upper crust arranges in order for their children to find spouses of a similar social class. We were both eighteen. I had maneuvered Jonathan Howard, the sixth son of the Marquess of Pembroke, into the coatroom. I had just managed to get a hand down the back of Johnny's trousers and was showing him some of the more mysterious parts of his anatomy when my future wife, Cornelia, fell through the door, wrapped in passionate embrace with Primrose Cavendish, the ninth child of the Duke of Devonshire."

I paused to see if Musa was horrified by my revelations,

but he was eying me with a slight grin. He took a sip of his drink and waved for me to continue.

"Johnny and Prim both just about died and fled the coat-room with such speed that I'm sure they could both have pursued careers in athletics if nobility didn't work out for them. I too, was scared, terrified that my secret would get out. But Cornelia looked me in the eye and then threw her head back with what I would soon come to know as her typical infectious abandon and laughed uproariously. In that second I knew that she was the woman I would marry.

"We were the first of our siblings on either side to be married and all of our brothers and sisters were nearly mad with jealousy and fear at our union. They'd all been so sure that neither of us would marry, and now we'd come from noth-ings to threats for their inheritance. Neither Cornelia nor I had any desire for any excessive sum, but we did both like children and we delighted at torturing our families, so as soon as we were married we decided that we needed a baby."

Again, I watched for Musa's reaction, and at the mention of a child he did raise an eyebrow. But I guess it wasn't too shocking, considering he'd already met the fruit of our ef-forts.

"However, as you know, it's only healthy for a child to be conceived out of love. Patient love at that, not rushed. And so, Cornelia and I set out to fall in love, if only for one night. We thought about dressing me up in ladies' clothing but it didn't work for either of us. So, Cornelia cut her hair short, which wasn't a problem as she'd inherited dozens of lavish hairpieces from her late mother, and went to the gymnasium to observe how men went about growing their muscles. Then she spent a few months exercising vigorously. I hated for her to do it, but she claimed to enjoy it. After a few months, on a dreary Wednesday evening, she let me see her naked and I must say that her effort was rather splendid. She insisted on me calling her Johnny—whom I did always view as a missed opportunity—and bent over on all fours. Nine months later we had Charlie!"

Now Musa looked a bit surprised.

"That can't be true," he said, smiling incredulously.

"It is! I swear it! And Cornelia liked the look so much that she kept it. She found it quite useful in attracting paramours. After Charlie was born, I can honestly say that we were in love. Unconventionally. Dangerously. But, in love. The only problem was that we'd both always wanted adventure, to travel and see the world, but we were frightened. London was dangerous enough for people like us. The rest of the world is even worse."

Musa nodded in vigorous agreement.

"Given our shared love—and lack—of adventure, I wasn't surprised when Cornelia fell head over heals for Abigail, the wife of a merchant we frequented at Borough Market. She was just Cornelia's type: gorgeous face, loose brown curls, bright blue eyes, a bawdy sense of humor—"

"You could be describing yourself," Musa said, his voice deep.

"But let me finish!" I laughed, my cheeks reddening. "I was about to say, 'with tits that could float her to Australia!'"

Musa snorted his whiskey and then wheezed. I shushed him, not wanting to wake Charlie, though I knew the boy would be sleeping for quite some time, given the combination of heat and alcohol.

"Anyway, Abigail and Cornelia began a rather torrid romance, either coming to our house or frolicking around at Abigail's when her husband was out of town. Then, one day, the police came to my door. They said that Cornelia and Abigail had both been found dead at Abigail's home, a bottle of strychnine clutched in Cornelia's hand. The police said it was a double suicide."

My voice had dropped to a whisper. I realized that I'd never once told the whole story to another soul. Musa put his hand on my leg. Nothing suggestive, just supportive.

"I am ashamed to admit that I believed the police. I thought that maybe they'd been so happy that they wanted to end it that way. I was so angry. I couldn't imagine how Cornelia could leave Charlie—and me! Though we didn't love each other like most couples, we did love each other. Perhaps even more deeply."

I took another sip of whiskey and continued.

"I would have stayed ignorant if the merchant—who was, as I suppose you've guessed by now, Ezekial Greyhorn—hadn't sent me that damned letter. It wasn't a letter of confession, nor of condolence. It was *conspiratorial!* As if we'd been in on it together. He *revealed* that our wives had been offending our masculinity through acts against God and nature, and he'd saved us both the humiliation by dispatching them. That was it. No apology, no shame."

I was shaking and Musa kept his hand on my leg. His grip was firm. He began to rub his thumb in small circles on my thigh and the feeling was calming.

"So I have resolved to kill him. To avenge her."

"Okay," Musa said quietly. "I'll tell you where he is. I've got business with him, so I'll even take you to him myself. But tell me something."

"What?"

"Why did you bring your son?" he asked.

I didn't even need to think.

"I brought Charlie along to see me do it, so that, even if he couldn't look up to his father as a man, he'd know I did the manly thing, if just this once."

"And murder is a manly thing?" Musa asked quietly.

I felt horribly bleak and didn't know how to express my thoughts clearly. Instead, I looked at his lips, which were thin and dark, almost blue, like ice. They were strangely inviting. I fell forward, pushing my lips against his.

He froze at first and I wondered if I'd guessed wrong. The signs all seemed to be there. Then he pushed his tongue into my mouth and grabbed my face, pushing deeper.

I put my hands between his legs, and when I felt what he had there, I made a noise of surprise. I'd heard the tales, of course, but hadn't expected them to be so accurate.

To my disappointment, Musa slapped my hand away and pushed his chair back, putting distance between us.

"I won't fulfill your fantasy of having some African savage brutalize you, if that's what you're after," he said, his voice dark and his eyes pained.

Of course not, I wanted to say. But then I wondered if that would be a lie. So instead of speaking, I stood up and walked to him, grabbing his hands and pulling him up too. Then I turned him around and pressed myself against his backside, biting him on the neck, holding his hands behind him.

He whirled around forcefully. "Oh, is it that what you want? To debase the unwilling slave? I won't do that for you either."

God, he was being difficult. But he was also right; I was fetishizing him. He was so foreign to me I didn't know what to do with him.

"I don't know how to do this," I said miserably.

"Stop thinking," he said. His face lightened. "Just slow down. You probably always do it in secret. Or in shame. Am I right?"

"Is that different here in Africa?" I said, surprised.

"For God's sake, no!" Musa laughed. "Are you kidding?"

I just stared at him.

"It is different with me, though."

And then he took me by the hand and led me into the bedroom.

We left most of our luggage at the Bender's Arms, bringing only one suitcase. I once again had the gun nestled into the waistband of my trousers, today concealed by a dark red waistcoat and my frock coat. Charlie was dressed in his Hussar suit, a miniature blue and gold Prussian military outfit with lines of braid across the chest. I'd told him that he'd need to be very brave on our journey and he'd insisted on wearing his bravest outfit in response.

Musa, dressed once again in tight trousers and a white collared shirt, led us to the train. I was used to taking the train in England and had expected its African cousin to suffer by comparison. Instead, it was beautiful. We were led to our own cabin in first class, where a steward told us that lunch would be served at twelve o'clock sharp. He also told us that the viewing car was open all day and there was the strong possibility that we would see wildlife if we watched from there.

Musa had informed me that Greyhorn was working out of the village of Kikuyu, where missionaries had set up a hospital some years before. Kikuyu, named for the predominant ethnic group in British East Africa, was twenty miles past Nairobi, in the shadows of Mount Suswa. It was over three hundred miles from Mombasa and would take us anywhere between eight and fifteen hours.

Once the train chug-a-lugged to life, Charlie ran for the viewing deck, eager to see animals. I told him that I'd join him soon but to come and check with me before every stop. I didn't want him to wander off the train and out into the African bush.

Once we were moving along in earnest, I turned to Musa, who was staring at me intently.

Disarmed, I was quiet for a moment. Then I finally asked, "So, how it is that you have a Scottish accent?"

"This isn't Scottish, it's African. A Kikuyu accent, I swear!"

I narrowed my eyes and he laughed.

"Here's the short version—" he began.

"Why the short version? We have all day," I said with a smile. It was mostly for show. In my mind, I knew that my destination was murder.

"It's the short version because I have things that I'd like to do with you that don't involve talking," he said.

I nodded. That was a good plan in my book.

"A while back, the Church of Scotland tried to mimic what was called a 'civilizing mission,' which was the kind of mission that the Portuguese and the Dutch established as far back as the sixteen hundreds. They founded a hospital in Kikuyu, where you and I are headed right now, and a school in Rabai, just north of Mombasa. I was a baby when they arrived, and that's what they were after. They took as many of us children—orphans, they said—as they could get and raised us like we were Scottish ourselves. We learned only English, went to church on Sundays, and were raised by nice white Christians who told us our parents had died of famine."

I nodded along, but was embarrassed to admit that I knew nothing of mission work. I thought it was an altruistic pastime for bored women at events, not an actual life-shaping industry.

"When I was fifteen, an awful influenza spread through the settlement that had built up around the school and its small clinic. All of the white people got it while most of the Africans were immune. It was ironic, considering how many diseases they'd brought with them when they arrived. The next thing we knew, the ones who survived jumped on a boat back to England, leaving the rest of us to fend for ourselves. Luckily, they'd left their supplies, too. So, those of us who were able packed up all of the medical equipment from the clinic, as well as all the medications they'd hoarded over the years. We loaded them onto the train and went to the mission hospital outside Kikuyu. As it turns out, they had been low on supplies for over a year. They paid us much more than double what our supplies were worth, and we remaining 'orphans' split the money amongst ourselves. I eventually came to Mombasa and bought the Bender's Arms. I have a friend who moved to a village on Lake Victoria and opened a restaurant. One girl bought a ticket to France. Another stuck around Mombasa for a while, helped me at the bar, and then married an Englishman and now lives outside Nairobi."

"At least something good came of it," I said, not knowing if he was happy about this or not.

"I was pretty happy until I told a customer my story one day. He said we'd all been stolen. Just snatched away from our families. None of them had died of famine. We'd just been taken, educated like Europeans, so that when we had kids we'd teach them to be like Europeans too."

"That's horrible," I said, and it was my turn to place a consoling hand on his leg.

He looked at my hand like he didn't know what to do with it, then smiled.

"It's fine. I wouldn't have ever bothered to learn Kikuyu and Swahili if he hadn't told me that. I wouldn't have tried to learn as much about my ancestors' culture as I could. So I'm on my way. I know how to speak like a European, but I also know how to fight them."

I wanted to tell him something significant and meaningful, but my mind was blank.

Instead, I kissed him: a nice, slow kiss, as opposed to the intense passions of the night before. I moved closer to him, but rocketed back as a knock sounded on the door.

It was Charlie, who was nothing if not polite. Thank God.

He was buzzing, hopping up and down like a little wild bee.

"I'm almost positive I saw five lions!" he squealed.

Considering we weren't yet out of Mombasa, I doubted it. Musa, bless him, smiled warmly and invited Charlie in to have a seat.

"Tell me all about them," he said, and Charlie beamed.

"Here it is," Musa said to me as he, Charlie, and I approached the small wooden house on the edge of Kikuyu. "Have a look in the window."

"Can you hold him?" I asked, passing Charlie, who had fallen asleep after a day of animal watching, over to Musa.

I pulled the pistol from the back of my trousers and approached the house. I peered in the window and saw him. Ezekial Greyhorn. The murderer. The villain.

Part of me wanted to raise the pistol to the window, pull the trigger, and just be done with it. But I wanted him to know what I was doing. And I wanted Charlie to see me kill him. I was about to turn around when I noticed the table behind Greyhorn and, seated at it, a beautiful, plump black woman. I watched her for a moment, saw her attempt to stand, and saw Greyhorn run over to stop her, probably telling her to rest. He put his hand on her swollen belly. And then turned around, the ghost of a smile on his face. He was going to be a father.

I spun around and hurried back to Musa.

"Did you know about the woman? About the baby?" I hissed.

"Yes," he said, meeting my eyes.

"Why didn't you tell me? She's your friend, isn't she? One of the Rabai orphans, Scottish and Kikuyu. The one who married the Englishman and now lives outside Nairobi!"

I was floundering. How could I widow someone? How could I take a parent away from his child?

Musa nodded slowly. "If I'd told you and you'd decided not to go, then you'd always wonder if I'd been telling the truth. You'd always regret doing nothing. And if I'd told you and you'd wanted to do it anyway, then I wouldn't have been able to look at you," he said.

I wanted so badly to tell him he was right. To turn and

head back. Maybe start some kind of life with him. What kind of life could we start? Secret, but less secret than back in London, perhaps. Charlie could grow up in Mombasa, in the sunshine, by the sea, surrounded by people of different backgrounds.

But I was going to disappoint them both.

"Take Charlie to the train for me," I asked. I had wanted Charlie to see me kill Greyhorn. But for him to see me kill him in front of his pregnant wife? No.

Musa looked surprised and took a step back.

"Nothing else. I have no other expectations. Just take him back there and watch him until I get there."

Musa looked sad and hurt. He nodded again, then turned around, taking the sleeping Charlie in his Hussar uniform with him.

I had wanted to do this thing to show Charlie what a man was, but that wasn't my reason any more.

I wanted to do this because of what Greyhorn would do to his unborn child if he or she grew up different. I wanted to do this because he would kill them if they wronged him or his God just as he had killed Abigail and Cornelia.

And what of his new love? What would he do to her when he realized that she wasn't Scottish on the inside, that she was different, too? I wanted to kill him for her.

But really, I needed to kill him because he had killed the

only woman I had ever loved. I didn't want to live in a world in which he still existed and she did not.

I needed to do it. All I had to do was pull the pistol from my pocket and rake my knuckles across the wooden door. I would see Greyhorn's eyes fall across my own, see the light of recognition. I would to raise my gun and shoot him in the face. Not cleanly. Messy. I would shoot off half his head and watch him slip to the ground like a windless kite. Then he'd be a matched set with poor James at the Bender's Arms. Together, they'd have a whole face.

I trudged back to the train station and found Musa on a bench with a sleeping Charlie sprawled across his lap. He didn't even look up, though he had to have heard me coming.

"I didn't do it," I whispered.

He stayed completely still for a moment and I wondered if he'd heard me. Then he looked up and his eyes were filled with kindness and perhaps surprise.

"What stopped you?" he said.

I wanted to say, "You did," and walk over and embrace him, to thank him for saving me. But it wasn't true and I couldn't lie about something like this.

"For Charlie. I've always been so concerned that someday he'll learn the truth about me and be ashamed. But how could he ever be anything but ashamed if I made myself into a murderer? Greyhorn will burn in hell when he dies, but it won't be by my hand."

Musa thought on that for a second and simply, comfortably, gripped my hand.

After a long moment I said, "Can we just get on the train and keep going west? Towards Lake Victoria? Someplace unknown?"

"I've got a bar to run," he said quietly, looking down the empty train tracks.

"Just give me a week. Give me a week to figure out what's next. What I want," I said, concerned by how it would all play out, but certain that I wanted Musa to be a part of it.

Musa looked up and smiled.

YEV

The cold blue sky laid above me, concealing my destination, as I sat crammed into the orbital module of Soyuz TM-M spacecraft that would be flying my team to the International Space Station. Once there, we would replace three of the six current crewmembers. All three of us would be on ISS for one hundred and eighty four days. Six months. Six months of floating around small compartments with strangers, eating hydrated, rehydrated, or tubed food, sleeping strapped in and tied to a wall, and washing myself with the equivalent of those little wet napkins they give you at barbecue joints. I was so excited I could barely breathe.

At thirty-four I was to be one of the youngest ever to enter outer space, the second youngest American after Sally Ride, who I was named after. Not Sally, which would have been an awful name for parents to give a son, but rather Rider, which in my opinion wasn't that much better. At my time of birth, both of my folks were physicists and feminists, so it was only natural that they'd name their firstborn son after the first woman in space.

We were launching from the Baikonur Cosmodrome in Kazakhstan. Our crew was made up of our commander, Brent Nalley, a handsome, fifty-something former Navy pilot who was making his fourth spaceflight, JAXA astronaut Kimiko Yoshida, a tall and muscular Japanese mechanical engineer making her second spaceflight, and myself, a biomedical engineer. Nalley and Yoshida would be joining the three remaining crewmembers on the ISS for a specific mission: to standardize the docking systems on the station in order to allow for more space tourism.

My mission was completely different, an oddity for the station. All crewmembers on the ISS are required to complete two hours of exercise a day to prevent muscle atrophy, depression, and other complications that come with being in an isolated space station for months at a time. My job was to update the two treadmills, weight machine, and exercise bike on the station and then to monitor the exercise of the other crewmembers over the next six months in order to make sure my upgrades has been sufficiently beneficial.

From the start, Nalley had been friendly but very formal. Distantly paternal. As the commander, he wanted everything on the station to be easy to manage, and that meant not getting too close to anyone. Having five crewmembers on one job and one on another was messy. Most of my interactions with him were technical, instructions on how to operate equipment. Though first time astronauts weren't at all unusual, I was especially inexperienced. I hadn't been in the military. My only connection to NASA had been that my parents had obsessively sent me to space camp as a teenager. Strangely, I would only be the second-ever space camp graduate in space. However, my research, which involved the effects of cardiovascular exertion on individuals in high-pressure situations, made me perfect for the kind of work that needed to be done on the ISS. Furthermore, I was in excellent physical condition and had made it through all of the necessary training simulations with ease.

So I could understand Nalley's keeping me at arm's length though I still wished I were embarking on this adventure alongside a friend. Yoshida was fine, but as a fellow engineer all she wanted to talk about was research, hypotheses, and equations. I wanted to talk about anything *but* work, considering we would be living and breathing it for six months. I wanted to talk about movies, or travel, or men. Well, I couldn't really talk with any of them about men, but it was one of my favorite topics of discussion.

I didn't hide my sexuality in my private life, but since getting the NASA contract I'd been hesitant to talk about it. I'd gotten the distinct impression from management that the ISS was one of the few areas where there was real, healthy collaboration between the US and Russia and any talk of homosexuality, public or private, could jeopardize that.

The activist in me wanted to fight it. And my ego did, too. There had never been an openly gay astronaut before. Sally Ride had been gay, but it hadn't become public knowledge until her death. I wanted to fly the rainbow flag for gay astronauts.

But the weird thing about being asked to go to outer space is that you're pretty much willing to agree to whatever they tell you. Less than six hundred people had ever even been to space. I wasn't going to give up the chance, even if it meant compromising a few of my principles.

Plus, maybe I needed a break from talking about love. Though I hate to admit it, I'd been killing my friends with laments about the end of my last relationship. Josh and I had seemed like a match made in heaven. Me, the brilliant engineering professor and him, the soccer coach at a big, liberal university. We'd been dating for two years when I'd come home early from a conference to find him plowing *my* teaching assistant, Bobby. He was fucking him so hard that it shook the dishes in our kitchen cabinets and my first thought had been, "He's never fucked *me* like that." My second thought had been that Bobby's only significant attributes were his Excel skills and his thick bubble butt. I had a bubble butt, a big dick, a PhD *and* a medical degree for God's sake. I'd kicked him out, fired Bobby, and spent the subsequent six months doing extra squats at the gym and moaning to my friends about Josh's betrayal.

I shook my head. I was about to fly into *outer space* and I was thinking about Josh. Again. I stared up, listening to Mission Control issuing instructions over the radio and Nalley responding to each command with a deep, clear, "affirmative." In the movies, it seemed like a pretty quick process. The astronauts showed up, got in place, and then they counted down from ten and shot you off into space. We'd been instructed that it was a bit different than that, but I was still surprised at how long we sat there sweating in our suits, waiting for every inch of the Soyuz to be inspected by both eye and computer.

All of the inspirational videos in the world can't make up for the fact that you are sitting on top of what is, more or less, a bomb. I couldn't help but think that at any moment, someone could make a mistake and we would all be consumed by a massive fireball. As an engineer, I both understood and trusted the machinery. It was the hundreds of humans working *with* the machinery that worried me.

I'd been through enough simulations to know what to expect, though, so when I heard the large mechanical arm that held the Soyuz in place disengage I knew that the explosion beneath us would follow within seconds. Even with the simulations, not to mention our state-of-the-art headsets, which absorbed enough of the sound to keep our eardrums from bursting, the explosion precipitating takeoff was a shock.

I have no idea how Nalley kept talking so calmly to Mission Control. I didn't even realize until we were already in the air that he was alternating between Russian and English. I would have been impressed if I hadn't been breathless with terror.

I had thought that at this point I would feel like a pioneer, one of the significant fewest of few who get a chance to make this journey. However, during that ascent from the Earth's surface I felt the opposite. As the blue sky became icier and thinner and eventually clear, giving way to gray and then black, I felt insignificant, tinier and tinier as we left the safety of home and hurled out into the great unknown.

We were in space in ten minutes. Nalley, like an outdoorsman on a hunting weekend, seemed twenty years younger.

"Welcome to outer space, ladies and gentlemen" he said to us through our headsets. I stared ahead in wonder as Nalley spoke to Mission Control. Yoshida yelled "Yeehaw!" and pumped a fist, which in our giant suits looked like the tiny wave of a marshmallow man.

Nalley pushed a button and then another in quick succession. I knew what he was doing, I had been trained as backup in case he was incapacitated (second back-up, actually, after Yoshida) but my mind was so detached that he looked to me like a dentist does to a recently gassed patient.

I was rocked back into awareness by a piercing "whoosh" which sent our entire module hurdling sideways, like the teacup ride at Disneyland. I shot a sideways look at Nalley in panic but then quickly recalled that this was the process for putting us into orbit. Once we were settled into orbit, we would then execute a series of Hohmann Transfers, which would, after a series of orbits around the Earth, line us up with the International Space Station. Ideally, this process would take about six hours, but it could take much longer if we weren't perfectly lined-up.

Nalley managed to get lined up with the station in almost exactly six hours, executing the Hohmann Transfers precisely. Each transfer involved a burn of our engines to push out of the current orbit and into a further one and then a brief counter-burn of engines on the opposite side to keep us in the new orbit. Nalley conducted this all so smoothly that I even slept a bit, despite the extraordinary situation. Adrenaline could only sustain me for so long and I hadn't slept a wink the night before.

When we were finally in-line with the station, we slowed down and let it catch up with us. The ISS rockets around the earth at an incredible speed, making a full orbit in ninety minutes. So we needed to maintain a fast enough pace so that it wouldn't just smash into us, but rather gain on us until we could connect with minimum impact.

Within minutes, we connected with the station. In simulations, it was a natural, Lego-like connection. In real life it was loud, shaky, and uncertain, a blind collision with a giant piece of metal moving at over seventeen thousand miles an hour.

Nalley's voice was calm and firm in his communication with Mission Control and so I tried to use his as a cue. But I also knew that he was trained to be calm at all times, even if we were headed for certain death.

Once our Soyuz was connected with the ISS, Nalley reached up and completed the manual side of the connection with ease and efficiency. Though Mission Control was guiding him through the steps, he seemed to know them perfectly anyway, his fingers moving confidently from button to handle to lever without any hesitation.

Finally, it was time to open the hatch door. I waited for Nalley to open the door and then said to Yoshida, "Ladies first."

Yoshida unbuckled and smiled brightly as she floated directly upward. She caught the hatch door, which couldn't open fully into our orbital module because of the various supplies wedged in with us, and then bent around it with lithe precision, like a deep-sea diver entering a sunken pirate ship.

"You're next, Rider," Nalley said to me. It was traditional for us to call each other by our last names, but as I was named after Sally they all called me Rider.

I unclipped and was immediately struck with the wonder of weightlessness. I'd experienced it in simulations, but to do it in space was a different animal. It was like a more natural form of swimming. I wound my way around the circular hatch door and into the Docking Compartment. I floated up through the narrow docking modules and into the Zarya Functional Cargo Block, the FCB, which more or less connected the US and Russian sections of the ISS. The American Node One, Unity, lay at one end and Russia's Zvezda Service Module at the other.

Yoshida was floating down through the FCB towards Unity. Beyond Unity was the Destiny, the US Lab, where I would be doing most of my data processing work, and beyond that was Node 2, Harmony. I expected that Yoshida was headed to Harmony, which was where her sleeping quarters were, though she could also be headed to Kibo, the Japanese Laboratory Module, which was just a quick left turn out of Harmony.

I turned the other way, looking towards Zvezda. Zvezda housed one of the two bathrooms on the ISS and, if Nalley and Yoshida were to be believed, the cleaner and less used of the two. And, after six hours in orbit, I really needed to pee.

Zvezda was also home to the sleeping quarters for the cosmonauts. Well, usually for the cosmonauts. Due to the nature of my assignment, I'd be sleeping in Zvezda. The typical personnel make-up of the ISS is two or three cosmonauts, two or three astronauts, and one or two others. There were never more than six people aboard. On our mission, however, there would be only one cosmonaut, the remaining Yevgeny Kulakov, who to my knowledge was trained as a pilot and as a civil engineer. His only colleague from Roscosmos, the Russian space agency, was rotating off of the station, along with two US astronauts. This left a Belgian biochemist from the European Space Agency (ESA), Leo De Vroom, a US physicist named Carla Williams, and then Nalley, Yoshida, and myself. Since Columbus (the ESA Lab), Destiny, and Kibo were down directly connected to Harmony and that's where De Vroom, Nalley, Williams, and Yoshida would be doing most of their respective work, it made sense for them to be there. While I'd be doing my data processing in Destiny I would actually doing most of work rotating between the four pieces of exercise equipment on the ISS. Two of those, an exercise bike and the treadmill, were in Zvezda. I'd have to float down to Node 3, Tranquility, to monitor the weight machine, and I'd monitor the other exercise bike while doing my data processing because it was also in Destiny.

I looked down to Zvezda to see two men floating amongst the various cords, metal doors, and monitors, chatting and laughing while sucking brown liquid out of small plastic pouches.

As I floated in they looked up. They were both large men, tall and muscular. At six feet, I knew that I was tall for an astronaut, but both of them were taller than me. One had dark hair and a round, flat face with a thick beard, smiling but otherwise expressionless.

The other was fair-skinned, blond, his skin smooth and his face hairless. His cheekbones were sharp and wide and his eyes were cold and blue. His lips were light pink and perfectly shaped. His biceps were bulging pleasantly out of his blue t-shirt, which was tucked into nicely tight black pants.

I felt a surge of interest despite my deep-space disorientation.

Then I saw how rigid the planes of his face were. Interest faded. Logic returned. My superiors had made it clear that a healthy professional distance was to be kept between all inhabitants of the ISS.

I reached out a hand to greet them but didn't realize the momentum caused from the action in zero gravity would send my whole body forward. I surged forward, floating directly into the blond.

He calmly let go of his packet and used one arm to reach up and grab a small bar to stabilize himself while using the other arm to grab me and stop my forward flight.

"Watch it," he said sharply.

His hand was large, his grip firm, and despite his dour expression, my body responded favorably to the touch. Hopefully he'd think the flush in my cheeks was embarrassment.

The dark-haired fellow laughed and patted me heavily on the back, pushing me into the blonde again.

The blonde shot his companion a chilly look and gave me a slight shove backwards. I caught a bar towards the ceiling and steadied myself.

"Coffee?" the dark haired guy asked, the laugh still in his thick, deep voice.

"Oh that would be awesome," I said.

"Awesome," he repeated in a flat, exaggerated American accent, chuckling loudly. "Very American word." His accent was heavy but his tone seemed friendly.

"Oh, sorry, I'm Rider Stevens."

"Pasha Yeltsin. No relation to Boris," he said with a laugh. "You need not worry."

The blond was busy pumping water from a panel in the

wall into a small plastic bag. I'd watched a training video about this and knew he was suctioning hot water into a plastic bag of freeze-dried coffee. He turned said, "Yevgeny Kulakov."

Pasha showed me the bathroom and graphically explained how to use the long tube to suction my business out. One would think that peeing into a hose would be easy enough, considering the familiarity I had with similarly shaped items, but it was a struggle.

After I'd negotiated the peeing hose, I looked in the mirror on the wall of the bathroom. I looked like hell. I'd cropped my reddish brown hair close to my head because zero gravity makes your hair stand on end, so that looked fine enough, but my green eyes were bloodshot and bleary and I must have drooled while we were doing the Hohmann Transfers because a thin white line ran from the corner of my mouth down my chin. Gorgeous.

I quickly freshened up with some small, antibacterial towels. I'd learned in training that these towels would be a vital part of my bathing ritual, as the shower and bathtub of Earth were replaced on ISS by these small towels, dry shampoo, and a small pressure hose.

When I emerged, Yeltsin and Kulakov were talking to Nalley.

Nalley looked up and down and said, "Well, you're not covered in piss, so you're already doing better than I did on my first trip."

He and the two Russians laughed. Kulakov handed me the bag of coffee.

"Careful," he said. "It will burn you."

In my mind, I imagined this to be a metaphor, though Kulakov did not seem the type for symbolic language.

Nalley tossed a bag to me. Well, whatever the space word for "tossed" would be. He floated it over.

It was my bag of personal items, a couple of changes of clothes and some family pictures. Mission Control would upload my files and everything onto a computer already on station and my tools for modifying the athletic equipment and monitoring my colleagues were still packed away in the service module of the Soyuz. They'd be unloaded in the next hour or so as the crew prepared their descent module.

Yeltsin gestured to a small compartment in the back left corner of the Zvezda.

"Got my things parceled away so is free for you to take, friend," he said in stiff English. I appreciated the effort, as my Russian was far worse than his English.

Kulakov pointed to back right corner. "That is my sleeping compartment, so we are neighbors," he said, still expressionless, his blue eyes pinning me back.

"So no snoring, please," he added.

He had less of an accent than Yeltsin, though there was still a definite Russian sound to his words, particularly his vowels. "Please" had come out in two syllables.

Yeltsin guffawed and I realized belatedly that "no snoring please" was Kulakov's version of a joke.

Nalley turned to me.

"I'm headed over to Harmony to get settled in. You get yourself set up and then Yev can show you around, or if he's busy, at least point you in my direction."

"Yev?"

The blond spoke up, again with little inflection. "Me. Yev. Americans have trouble with Russian names so we like to keep them simple for you."

Once again, Yeltsin laughed, and even Nalley smiled. I faked a smile even though I disliked being the butt of a joke.

Nalley left, occasionally doing a somersault in the zero gravity as he proceeded through the FCB toward Unity and Harmony. He was in his element.

Yeltsin went to find Harry Zindall and Wendy Simtak-Hidenberg, the two astronauts who would be rotating off with him. They'd empty the Soyuz's service module of our equipment and then prepare their descent module. It was a tight turnaround, and despite his pleasant demeanor I could tell that Yeltsin was anxious.

Who wouldn't be? In just a couple of hours he'd be rocketing towards the surface of the earth at seven-hundred-and-fifty-five feet per second.

Yev apparently wasn't interested in small talk, as he turned away and floated over to a computer mounted on Zvezda's wall.

I unpacked my meager belongings, placing them carefully into my sleeping quarters. The sleeping quarters were bigger than I'd imagined, roughly the size of a telephone booth. On the wall to the left was a kind of wall-mounted vest, which I would hook myself into for sleeping. I could attach a sleeping bag to the bottom of it if I got cold, but I run hot so I didn't think that was going to be necessary. The space station stays about seventy-five degrees pretty consistently.

On the wall opposite the sleeping apparatus was a wall-mounted laptop, which I would use to communicate with Mission Control, to call home, to check emails, and to watch television. We had a surprisingly fast Internet connection on the ISS, but Mission Control would see everything I did so I didn't think I'd be doing a ton of personal surfing.

The wall directly across from the entrance had a small window, and I felt extra special, because the sleeping units in Harmony didn't. The view outside the window sent quick, unexpected tears to my eyes. The hair on my arms stood on end.

It was Earth. This was my first view of the Earth from the ISS. There is no appropriate way to describe the feeling of seeing the Earth from outside of it. I suppose it's like an out-of-body experience, like watching yourself on the operating table from the ceiling of the emergency room. The maternal blue curve of the Earth against the black of space called to me.

I felt a quick, sharp longing, a *need* to be back there, back in the Earth's safe embrace.

More tears came, and I must have made some sort of noise because a hand gently grabbed my shoulder, turning me around.

It was Yev; his eyes still cold, his body rigid. He saw my wet eyes and then looked beyond me, to my view of Earth, and his eyes softened. The change, though just a millimeter of skin, was monumental.

Liquid had rolled off of my face as I turned and now floated between us, an asteroid belt of tears. I was embarrassed but also at a loss for how to hide my emotion.

"Your first look?" he said, his hand still on my shoulder.

"I saw it from the Soyuz, but that was different somehow."

"Yes. I. . ." He was thinking, looking for the right words. "I think it calls you back, somehow."

Then, as quickly as he'd arrived, he let go and turned away, and I was disturbed by how significant the departure of his hand felt.

Yev didn't give me a tour. He was extremely busy; as the only civic engineer onboard, he would be overseeing the actual

logistics of the current mission, though Nalley was techni-
cally in command. Yoshida did the honors. It was a quick
tour, and served more as an opportunity for me to practice
my movement in zero gravity than as an actual tour. We
skipped a couple of areas that weren't functionally important, such as the new viewing deck, an Italian contribution.

I had a surprisingly tasty dinner of rehydrated beef tips and
asparagus with Williams, Yoshida, and De Vroom. Yev ate si-
lently in front of the small television next to his workstation in
Zvezda and Nalley was busy taking inventory of all of the supplies Yeltsin, Zindall, and Simtak-Hidenberg had unloaded
before departing. They'd left about an hour after we'd arrived
without ceremony, just a few quick hugs and handshakes.

De Vroom was a stocky, bald man with big bug eyes and a
constant smile. He'd been a gymnast in his youth and delighted in showing off his (admittedly impressive) zero
gravity moves. Williams was striking because of her mane of
black curls that floated like a school of fish above her head
and because her dark skin stood out so starkly against the
metal and white walls of the ISS.

I found De Vroom and Williams to be easy company and I
was instantly thankful. Aside from Yev, the rest of the team
was friendly and easygoing. Yoshida was a bit stiff and De
Vroom a bit exuberant, but neither of those were unforgiv-
able sins.

After dinner, Williams and De Vroom returned to their workstations in Destiny and Columbus, respectively, while Yoshida went to get set up in Kibo. Nalley handed me my toolkit, which I'd be using to adjust each of the four pieces of exercise equipment over the next week.

At 19:30 on the dot we began what Nalley called "pre-sleep activities" and this included everything from bathing to watching television to Skyping home. While Nalley used the bathing area, I called my folks, who were breathless with excitement and toasted me with champagne from their retirement home in Santa Fe. My two younger brothers were there, too. They'd had a little party to toast the launch. An unexpected surge of homesickness sliced through me, and I pushed it away.

When I finished the call I emerged from my sleeping quarters to see if Yev had finished. I came out just in time to see him emerge, wearing nothing but a small pair of black shorts.

The first thing I noticed was how smooth and perfect his skin was. It looked painted. His nipples looked almost red on his pale chest, which was large, round and strong. His abdominal muscles were almost comically defined. There was a light line of blond hair running down from his belly button down into his shorts, and I followed the line with my eyes, my breath quickening. He didn't appear to be wearing underwear and the front of his shorts appeared to be full. Very full.

His hips were slim, or maybe just appeared slim because they were between the breadth of his shoulders and the strong muscles of his legs.

He was glistening, and his hair was adorably mussed by the no-rinse shampoo we were required to use on the ISS.

I'd been so busy raking my eyes up and down his body that I hadn't realized he was staring right back at me, an eyebrow raised.

He said nothing, just stared, and I knew I should think of some excuse.

"I see you're in excellent shape, Yev," I said, clearing my throat. "Once I adjust the exercise equipment, I'll make sure that you're even better off."

It *was* a part of my job to monitor his body, wasn't it?

Yev just continued to stare, his cold eyes pinning me in place. What was I doing? Sexually harassing a colleague on my first day on the job? This was horrifying.

His mouth curled in a weird smile. His face seemed to fight it. As his lip curled, he asked, "Do you need help with the shower?"

The way he asked seemed cruel somehow, which made absolutely no sense, but that's what I felt.

And, more importantly, was he propositioning me?

"Hmmm?" was all I could muster.

"The shower. It is strange the first time. It's more of a—

what would you call it—a squirt gun? Do you need me to show you how to operate it?"

Oh. He was literally asking me if I needed help with the shower. Not like, "Let's take a sexy zero-gravity shower together" but rather like "You seem awfully stupid, let me show you how to use a squirt gun."

"I should be fine," I said, hoping my cheeks weren't turning red.

"Okay. Well, I will be in my sleeping quarters. Lights out is 21:30."

"Affirmative," I said with a small salute.

He stared for a minute, then turned and floated into his small sleeping unit.

✶

I spent the next week upgrading the exercise equipment. As a result of their time in zero gravity, astronauts on the ISS struggled with muscle atrophy and decreased bone density even with two scheduled hours of exercise every day. My hypothesis back on Earth had been that we were actually contributing to this by not giving the astronauts' muscles enough time to recover between workouts. NASA's trainers had been prescribing high-weight, low rep weights, high resistance biking, and interval running in order to build muscle faster than the astronauts were losing it. However, because of the difference in the amount of oxygen getting to the muscles on the ISS versus Earth, their muscles weren't recovering in enough time to build and were rather being worn down by both the lack of gravity *and* the workouts.

My team's solution had been to suggest alternating these high-intensity workouts with endurance-building workouts. Unfortunately, the equipment wasn't programmed for that. The settings on the treadmills, the bike, and the weight machine were skewed towards heavy, intense workouts.

It was a slow week. I needed to do my repairs in the periods of time where no one was scheduled to be using them, and with six people doing hour-long rotations twice a day it was a complicated task to organize my work so that the machines were all usable when people needed them. Luckily, my team had devised the schedule back on Earth and I'd practiced hundreds of times, so I was ready. What I wasn't ready for was the isolation. While the others went back and forth between laboratories and meals and exercise routines, the structure of my schedule meant that during the workday I was almost always alone. I only saw people at breakfast. I ended up eating lunch while the others were either exercising or working, and I had to work on the Resistive Exercise Device (RED) in the evenings while the others ate dinner because I needed more than just an hour at a time to make the necessary upgrades to it.

I saw Yev most of all, which was a worst-case scenario. In

the mornings, he demanded silence while he watched the Russian news over his coffee. And in the evenings, he hogged our small bathing area for most of the time and then either lurked grumpily is Zvezda's communal area or disappeared into his sleeping quarters.

Occasionally, I'd hear him in his quarters speaking in quiet Russian. Our quarters in Zvezda had thinner walls than those in Harmony, so it wasn't like I was *trying* to overhear him. My knowledge of Russian was rudimentary, so I missed most of what he said, but occasionally I would hear him end calls with "I miss you, too."

I wondered if Yev was married. Despite his personality, he'd make quite the catch. Being a cosmonaut was incredibly respected in Russia, and this was Yev's third spaceflight. He was also attractive, and I knew from his file that he was young, thirty-seven.

But I couldn't imagine Yev being romantic. His face was almost always blank, and it was impossible to imagine him showing passion or even humor. I thought back to his weird, uncomfortable attempt at a smile. Who could fall for that?

But then, deep in the night, I would lay (float?) in my sleeping unit, unable to forget the fact that his smooth, muscular body was literally inches from mine, on the other side of a thin metal wall.

On my final evening of upgrades, I went to work on the

RED while the others ate. I was getting pretty good at floating through the ISS. Between my years spent swimming competitively in high school and college and the NASA simulations, I was well trained in low-gravity movement. I floated down to Tranquility, my tools strapped around my waist.

When I got to Tranquility, I found Yev strapped into the RED, preparing to push the heavily weighted resistance bar forward.

I was annoyed; I'd been clear to everyone that I needed to work on RED in the evenings. I was about to voice my displeasure, but then Yev pushed forward on the bar, and the muscles in his arms coiled outward, graceful and strong, like twin cobras. His face showed minimal exertion as he pushed, and then as he allowed the bar to come back towards his chest, his arms tensed, his biceps swelling almost-obscenely outward.

My mouth was dry and I couldn't help but imagine myself wrapped in those arms, Yev pulling me towards him.

Just as my mind went there, Yev turned to me, his face blank.

"Sorry, I was just taking a quick break. I'll get out of your way," he said, beginning to unstrap himself.

I cleared my throat. "No, I don't need to start for a few minutes. I'll just look at the COLBERT," I told him. "Keep going."

He smiled, once again seeming to fight against his face to do so.

The COLBERT was the second treadmill on the ISS. The

letters stand for Combined Operational Load Bearing External Resistance Treadmill, but it's actually named after Stephen Colbert, late night television host. There had been a public vote to name Node 3, and the name Colbert won. However, NASA had reserved the right to reject any name it didn't find appropriate, and Node 3 was instead named Tranquility after the Sea of Tranquility, the section of the Moon where Apollo 11 landed in 1969. To appease outraged Colbert fans, NASA named the treadmill after him.

I'd finished adjusting the COLBERT the day before, but it couldn't hurt to check it one more time before I had to start monitoring individuals. I floated over to the COLBERT, but turned and worked while facing Yev.

He continued to slide the heavy bar forward and back, and his steady, pumping rhythm made me breathless. I tried to focus on the COLBERT, but I couldn't stop staring at Yev.

If he minded, he kept it to himself. Instead, he told me that he'd been working in Tranquility all afternoon, taking measurements. Tranquility had six berthing ports, but only three were in use. It was Yev's job to determine whether it was viable to upgrade any of the three unused berthing ports in order to accommodate space tourism. He'd gotten bored and decided to exercise a bit to break up the monotony.

I logged into the COLBERT and double-checked that the exercise plans I'd programmed in were available and ready for use. They were. I continued to sneak looks at Yev's pumping biceps as I worked, and I was disappointed when he exhaled heavily and then began to unstrap himself from the RED.

He wasn't even sweating, though I'd noticed that he'd had the resistance set on a level higher than even Nalley and I used, and our two programs involved the most simulated weightlifting. Yev's was a bit less because he would be doing more spacewalks than any other crewmember, so his Roscosmos personal trainer had devised a slightly less rigorous program.

"Are you sure you should be lifting so much?" I asked.

Yev looked at me, face granite, his blue eyes unreadable. "Don't worry, doc."

He said "Doc" like it didn't fit into his mouth correctly.

He rose. He was wearing a light blue t-shirt that brought out his eyes and was tight enough to suggest the muscle shifting beneath.

Yev looked at me and then looked up over his head. When his eyes returned to mine, his expression had changed. Small lines had bunched around his eyes, and his lips were parted slightly, showing a bit of his shiny white teeth. He looked, almost, excited.

"Have you been to the Cupola?" he asked.

Cupola. I knew that I should know what that was, but my mind was cloudy. Images of Yev rhythmically pumping his arms up and down alternated with what was before me, his cold blue eyes, leaving me mindless and titillated.

"What?" was all I could muster.

"The Cupola. The viewing deck." He pointed over our heads. "It's up there. Come."

He grabbed my arm and I felt the connection viscerally. I'd had no human contact since he'd grabbed my shoulder on that first day.

He pushed off from the floor and we floated upward. We got to the circular entrance above us and Yev backed away.

"You first," he said, gesturing upward. "I was just up there, so the shutters are open."

I smiled at him, I'm not sure why, and then grabbed the edge of the Cupola's entrance and pulled myself upward. I looked ahead as I did and I was instantly struck with wonder.

The portholes that allowed us to look out from the rest of the station were, at most, twenty inches across. The Cupola's seven windows, a circular central window surrounded by six quadrilateral windows arranged around it in a hexagon, took up an entire wall. We were above one of the Earth's oceans and the sun was hitting it from behind us, making it the most bright and inviting shining blue.

I stared in awe as we swept along. I momentarily forgot I was in a station, and instead felt as if I were floating in space above the Earth, staring down from the stars.

I sensed Yev float up behind me. He put his hands on my shoulders. It made me almost as breathless as the view.

His grip was firm. I hoped and feared that he was embracing me, but I knew that it was more likely to Yev a gruffly masculine grip, like a trainer massaging a boxer.

"Beautiful," he said, his mouth closer to my ear than I'd expected.

I watched light play across the ocean, watched a weather formation swirl gently above it, and had to agree.

"This view is amazing. Thank you."

Yev pulled my left shoulder back and pushed my right shoulder forward, sending me into a gentle spin. I went with it, still in a stupor from the combination of the view and my barely contained lust for Yev.

When I'd gone one hundred and eighty degrees Yev grabbed my shoulders straight on. We were facing each other, only about six inches apart.

His face had once again traveled that millimeter to softness, and the change was just as lovely as the ocean below us.

"No, I meant you."

What did he mean about me? I looked at him in confusion, still confounded at how his cold eyes and rigid mouth could shift ever so slightly and transform him into a warm-faced dreamboat.

Wait, what had we been talking about? Hadn't he said

beautiful? Was he calling me beautiful? Surely not. Was that a compliment? Did he think I looked like a woman?

The confusion must have registered in my face.

His face closed off again, frosting over, and he said, "Sorry, I thought . . .You'll have to excuse me."

He put a hand to the ceiling to push himself back down towards Tranquility.

Well, fuck it.

Before he could move, I grabbed his face and pulled him towards me. We collided, open mouthed, but as soon as our lips connected and I felt the warmth of his mouth on mine, we were knocked back. The momentum I'd used to pull him towards me had knocked us away from each other after we'd collided.

Yev began to laugh. Then he reached his hand back up to the ceiling and my heart sunk. How could he leave after that?

But instead of pushing himself downward, he grabbed a stabilizing bar. He held himself in place and reached his other arm out to me, pulling me in. He wrapped the arm around my waist, holding me in place as he held himself in place with the other. Then he put his mouth on mine.

I opened up to him without hesitation, our tongues gently touching. It was a soft, slow kiss. I hadn't realized just how much I wanted Yev until I had him right there. I relished his muscled arm around my waist, his sturdy chest against mine. He took his time with the kiss and kept his eyes open, staring right into mine.

The movement of it was different than a normal kiss. The more forcefully we pulled towards one another the harder we were pushed back, so we had to continue at a slow pace. It was excruciating but mesmerizing. Every connection of lips, ever brush of tongue felt entirely intentional. I was conscious of every single attentive move Yev made.

It shocked me how someone who appeared so cold could make me feel so incredibly wanted in just a matter of seconds. He pulled me in harder and my right hip pressed into his crotch, and his excitement became even more palpable.

I reached a hand down and grabbed him through his pants. What was I doing? I couldn't think. I was *working*. I couldn't be doing this at work. Or could I?

He pulled back. He looked into my eyes and smiled, the first genuine smile I'd seen on his face, a free smile.

"Not here," he said. "We have time."

I lifted my hand and placed it on his face and pulled him back into the kiss.

We stayed up in the Cupola for another thirty minutes, slowly kissing in a loose embrace. I finally had to break the kiss, because I had to make adjustments to the RED or I risked throwing off my entire schedule.

Yev smiled another one of those real, impossible smiles at

me and went off to get dinner. I made my adjustments to the RED and then went to feed myself. Yev was done by then and I ate rehydrated chicken piccata and green beans alone, struggling to believe that my time with Yev in the Cupola had actually happened.

On my way back to Zvezda, I floated past Nalley, who was in the FCB doing inventory for an upcoming spacewalk.

"What's got you smiling, Rider?" he asked in his typical fatherly manner.

I didn't know I was smiling.

I stared at him for a moment and then recovered.

"Got all of the equipment upgraded, right on time."

"Good man," he said. "How's bunking down in Zvezda going? Kulakov not too frigid for you?"

"No . . . I mean, yes, he's a bit distant, but nothing I can't handle, sir."

"Good to hear. He's pissed off every member of every crew he's been on at some point, but he's a brilliant engineer. Truthfully though I think the guys at Roscosmos would rather have him out in space than down there with them," he said conspiratorially.

I'd have to send them a thank you note.

"Well, don't worry about me, sir. I grew up with two younger brothers, I know how to deal with grumpy men in close quarters."

"Very good, Rider."

He returned to his work, and I continued down through the FCB and into Zvezda. Yev's door was closed and I heard his voice, a low rumble, talking on the other side. I listened, trying to pick out phrases.

I could recognize a few words here and there but it wasn't until he said, "I love you, too," that I made out an entire phrase.

My cheeks burned hot and I suddenly felt sick. Did Yev have a boyfriend? Or a girlfriend? Or something even more serious? I hadn't asked. And though I'd accessed everyone's medical files in order to prepare for the tests I had to run, I'd not looked up any personal information on him.

The call seemed to end and I moved away from his door quickly, sliding into the bathing area and pulling the screen closed behind me.

I cleaned up with the dry shampoo, soap and the squirt gun and then brushed my teeth, swallowing the chalky toothpaste. I wanted to kick myself for getting so lost in my attraction to Yev. As someone who'd been cheated on, I didn't want to be a part in anyone else's heartbreak.

I spent as long as I could in the bathing area, but any longer would look at the least wasteful and at most suspicious. I pulled on a pair of gym shorts and poked my head out. Yev's door was closed. I floated by and swept into my own, thankful to have some time think.

I slid my arms through the sleeves on the wall of my sleeping quarters, steadying myself against the wall, floating in place. I closed my eyes and tried to think over my to-do list, but all I could see behind the lids of my eyes was Yev's face. I saw that miniscule change that transformed him from cold machine into prince charming over and over again. I could almost feel his mouth on mine, his tongue pushing into my mouth.

This was not what I was supposed to be thinking about.

I was trying to mentally trace over my schedule for the next day when I heard a tap on the door of my sleeping unit.

The ISS makes plenty of creaking and clicking noises at all times, but I couldn't even trick myself into thinking this was one of them.

"What?" I whispered, trying to hold onto my conviction.

"It's me. Let me in."

It was Yev, and now my body betrayed me, the hard consonants of his Russian accent sending electric pulses straight to my crotch.

I needed to tell him no. I needed more time to think about this. None of this was smart. Even if he wasn't involved with someone, and it sounded like he was, getting involved with a coworker was not only against the rules, it was emotionally dangerous.

But I couldn't fight it. I reached down and slid the door open.

Yev slid in, again wearing only those small black shorts. In the dim light, he looked perfect, like diagram of what a man is meant to look like. His muscles were hard and soft all at once, his skin smooth and warm.

There was barely enough room in the small unit for both of us. He was only about six inches in front of me. I was still in the vest connected to the wall, held in place, but Yev had to reach up to the ceiling to hold himself in place. He slid the door shut.

His face was unreadable, but I could feel the heat of his body. He put his hand on my chin and looked into my eyes. As he did, it softened, and I saw not only lust but what also looked like genuine affection.

"You know, at first I was pretty sure you didn't like me," I whispered.

I thought he'd smile, but instead he stiffened.

"I gave you coffee. That was nice, no?"

I laughed and he just stared at me, looking confused. I crossed the distance between us and planted my lips on his. His look brightened but then he was pushed back by the force of my kiss, his head hitting my computer.

"Ow."

"Oh shoot! Sorry."

"I've not done this before," he said with a nervous smile. "I don't know that anyone has done this before."

It was like he was asking for permission. I gave it, grabbing him gently behind the neck and pulling him to me.

This time I held us in place as we kissed.

Suddenly I remembered what had been bothering me before.

Breaking the kiss, I looked him in the eye and, feeling stupid, asked, "Do you have a, um, partner? Like a romantic partner?"

Yev popped an eyebrow up.

"Like a girlfriend?"

"Or a boyfriend," I said.

"I'm not gay," he said firmly.

I laughed, but his expression darkened.

"Oh," was all I could think to say. "But, what is . . .well, what is this?"

"I'm Russian. You can't be Russian and gay."

"But, you're interested in this. In me, right?"

Why did I sound so insecure?

He pushed his pelvis forward.

"Yes, I'm interested," he said, smiling slowly.

Then he added, "It's because you have nice breasts."

I gaped at him.

"I do *not* have breasts. These are pecs. They're hard. Look." I flexed.

He grabbed my chest with his hands and it felt wonderful, despite the irritating subject matter.

He rubbed my chest in a circular pattern. "Either way, very nice."

I was rock hard. I thrust my hips forward, my crotch connecting with his.

"And what about *that*? Women don't have that."

His eyes moved upward, as if he was debating something in his head.

"I guess so. I have one too, which I quite like, so it will be easy to like yours, too."

He apparently had enough of the chatting because then he kissed me, hard, grabbing my shoulders and holding himself in place.

I broke the kiss again.

"Okay, so no boyfriend. But do you have a girlfriend? A wife?"

His face hardened yet again.

"What do you think of me that I would do this if I was with someone else? I didn't ask you these questions because I thought I knew you to be honorable," he said.

My cheeks burnt. I looked down.

"I'm sorry. It's just, I overheard you saying 'I love you' on the phone and it made me worry."

His voice was cold. "You listened to my calls?"

"Um, no, I just overheard . . ."

This was all going horribly. I looked up at him and was

shocked to see a big grin on his face.

"Just joking. These walls are thin. I can hear all of your calls. Your mother calls you 'Ridey.' You need to get headphones so I don't have to hear such things."

I let out a breath of relief.

"And no, I have no girlfriend. Or wife. No sweetheart of either sex. And I don't want one. I say 'I miss you' and 'I love you' to my grandmother, who I call every evening. She raised me."

Suddenly I felt like an asshole. And why was I so disappointed that he didn't 'want' a 'sweetheart?' Also, who says *sweetheart*?

"Yev, I'm sorry. I don't know why I didn't . . ."

He interrupted me with a short, soft kiss.

Then he said, "You're very clumsy with words. It's very attractive to me, although I don't know why."

Then he began kissing me in earnest. It accelerated from being kissed for the sake of kissing into kissing that suggested something more.

The sleeping vest kept me moored to the wall and Yev took advantage of that, using my shoulders to hold himself in place while we kissed. His mouth moved down to my neck and then to my chest.

My chest felt especially exposed with my arms hooked into the vest, and Yev took advantage, licking each nipple slowly. I let out a low moan, almost a growl, and he looked up and smiled.

What followed was an acrobatic display the likes of which may never be matched on Earth or in space. After, we cleaned up, and then Yev wordlessly followed me back to my sleeping unit. I would have been surprised, except I realized I was expecting him to do it.

It was odd, sleeping with someone else in zero gravity, but it was also wonderful. Space was a lonely place and having Yev's warmth wrapped around me was sexy and comforting.

We continued like that, almost every night—and some afternoons—for the next three months. We did well to keep it a secret, though I'm pretty sure Williams caught on. And Nalley knew everything that happened on board, so I would be surprised if he hadn't even guessed, but no one said anything.

Then the week before he was supposed to leave, to head back to Earth, Yev pulled me into his sleeping unit just after breakfast.

"I need to ask you something before I go," he said, serious.

I couldn't deal with it. I had been in denial that this perfect thing we had here would come to end. I didn't want him to say anything. I really didn't want him to end things, but I also didn't want him to make a promise he couldn't keep. He'd made it clear he didn't want a 'sweetheart.' I could feel it. He would get my hopes up, and I'd be here for three months, waiting to see him back on Earth, and he wouldn't be there when I landed.

"People say all sorts of things when they're leaving."

"Stop it. I'm not *people*. I'm me. I'm not who you want me to be. I'm not gay, I'm not straight either, I guess. But I want to tell you I lied."

My stomach dropped.

"You lied?"

Then he laughed.

I was about to punch him. "Are you laughing at me?"

"Stop screeching. Yes, I'm laughing at you."

I was definitely going to punch him.

He continued, "I'm laughing because you look so sad. I lied, but not on purpose. But when you asked if I was seeing someone on earth . . ."

My stomach dropped. I was aiding and abetting a cheater. I stayed as still as I could in zero gravity, waiting for the other shoe to drop.

"And I said I didn't want one. And I didn't. But, I do want you. I want to be with you. I didn't realize at the time, but I've smiled more in the last three months than I have in the last thirty years. I've never wanted to be with anyone more than I want to be with you. I never have."

He said all of this with a stern, hard face. In the movies, it's usually a bit more passionate. But in the movies people aren't usually floating. I found myself wondering if I'd heard right.

"Wait, so . . .what does this mean?"

"Will you be with me when you land?"

"You mean like, with you geographically?"

He sighed. "You are making this very difficult, Rider. Please be with me. Like, my sweetheart?"

As he said it, his eyes thawed in that miniscule way, and I felt, somehow, like the most wanted man in the universe.

"Boyfriend?" I asked. "You want to be my boyfriend?"

He winced, but then broke into a smile. "Yes, will you be my boyfriend? Can you be thirty-seven and someone's boyfriend?"

I laughed, disbelieving the change in him. "I'm only thirty-four. I think that's the limit."

He smiled. "So, you'll be my boyfriend and I'll be your sweetheart?"

Sweetheart. Ugh. I laughed. "Sure. Yes. Yes!" I kissed him, making sure to hold onto his shirt so that we didn't float apart.

The terror I felt as I rocketed towards Earth at seven-hundred-and-fifty-five feet per second was matched by my fear that my boyfriend wouldn't be waiting for me when I landed.

We'd Skyped once a week since he'd landed on Earth, but Skyping with Yev was like calling information.

"Tell me about your week," I mistakenly asked once.

"I worked. I exercised five times. In the gym, it's very cold in Moscow. It reached negative thirty-one degrees centigrade on Thursday during the day. I visited my grandmother. I met with several government officials who wanted a picture with a cosmonaut. I also watched a television program. It was about a crazy family in Texas. Have you heard of it?"

"You watched *Dallas*?"

"Yes! *Dallas.* Very good. And I slept well. How has your week been?"

Still, he'd said he'd be there, at the Baikonur Cosmodrome, where we'd be transported after they collected our descent module from wherever we landed in Central Asia. And he said he had a surprise. We were supposed to be landing relatively close, but launching yourself at the Earth in a manmade meteorite was less of a precise science than I had anticipated.

Yoshida, Nalley, and myself were squeezed together in the descent module, which made the orbital module seem like a 747 by comparison. We'd simulated this, of course, but it had been over six months ago, so as we freefell before our parachutes opened, I screamed like a little girl. It was like being on the downward hill of a roller coaster for eight straight minutes.

After eight minutes, our first parachute opened, cutting our speed by two-thirds, which was still really freaking fast.

We swept along at that rate for fifteen minutes, during

which I managed to get my screaming in check. We were packed in so tightly that it was difficult for me to turn to see Yoshida or Nalley, which was a good thing considering they were probably glaring at me.

Finally, our last parachute opened, and we slowed to twenty-four feet per second. This was still too fast to land; we probably wouldn't die if we hit at this speed but it would suck a lot. In the final seconds before landing, the blessed engines on the bottom of our module fired up and ensured a relatively soft landing.

"Welcome back home, ladies and gentlemen," Nalley said through the headset.

✳

I had vowed to act cool, but when our van pulled up to the Baikonur Cosmodrome I just couldn't take it anymore. I swung the door open and jumped out, looking into the crowd of Roscosmos, JAXA, and NASA staff present to welcome us back.

Yev was there.

He was hard to miss, his pale skin glowing in the clear Kazakhstani sun. When he saw me, his eyes went wide and the smile took over his whole face. I couldn't help but think back to the first smile I'd seen from him, that pinched, alien looking shudder of his face. The fact that I had even a tiny part in opening him up warmed my heart.

I knew I was supposed to be calm. Go up and shake his hand, maybe give him a manly hug. We could embrace behind closed doors. But I slipped into some kind of animal state when I saw him. Logic left.

I barely registered the surprise in his eyes as I ran at him. I crossed the twenty feet between us in seconds and jumped into his arms, wrapping my legs around his waist.

His hands came up and grabbed my ass, holding me up, and when I kissed him square on the mouth I could feel his smile beneath my lips, feel him open up and kiss me back.

Cheers erupted and I realized they were cheering for us. We were surrounded.

Sense returned, I flushed and hopped down. To my surprise, Yev slid his arms up as I descended and enveloped me in his arms.

"You're much heavier on Earth," Yev said as he hugged me tight.

I broke the hug and turned around. Yoshida was staring at us, her mouth gaping open in shock. Nalley, to my surprise, was looking at his boots, obviously trying to suppress a smile.

"We're going to be in so much trouble," I said to Yev.

"No we're not," he said. "Well, maybe you. I quit."

I looked up at him in surprise.

"You quit? Why?"

Yev smiled, but he looked nervous.

"I am moving to America. With my," his voice dropped to a whisper, "boyfriend."

He let that sit for a second while I just stared at him, gaping. His blonde hair, longer now, whipped about in the wind.

"If that's okay?" he asked, his cheeks flushing.

I kissed him hard. Then, pulling back, "Of course that's *okay*. That's amazing."

"Great. Well, go, get checked in and have your medical and everything. Then, our first real date."

"Date? Where are we going?" I asked.

Yev's eyes narrowed and his hungry look quickened my pulse.

"A bed."

La Castaña

Depending on who was asking, Guy Harris called himself an aviator, a pilot, or a soldier of fortune. He used *aviator* when he was looking for work. *Pilot* he'd say if he didn't care much about the conversation. If he ran into a man like himself, a man who was "that way," that's when Guy was a *soldier of fortune.*

It was July of 1930, and Guy was in Panama City, en route to Venezuela, where the American Museum of Natural History was paying top dollar for pilots to fly over the Gran Sábana, a massive, unexplored grassland. The museum said their goal was to map the region for "scientific evaluation," but the dollars they were offering said they were looking for oil. That didn't matter to Guy. They'd be paying him for his flying, not his opinions.

Guy was taking a leisurely route south from Oklahoma down to Ciudad Bolívar, which would be his base in Venezuela. He'd bought the Metal Aircraft Corp G-2-W Flamingo right off the field at the National Air Races in Cleveland. It had been piloted by Elinor Smith herself, and Guy had reveled in her shock when he'd handed over the biggest bag of sugar she'd ever seen, twenty-five thousand dollars. Guy wasn't rich, but he needed a plane. He'd lost his first (and a piece of his heart) some months before. Then his daddy had died, leaving him enough to buy the Flamingo and still have cash left to start over again. So he'd spent the money on something the old man had loved—and flying was the only thing his daddy had ever loved.

Guy had already stopped in Brownsville, Mexico City, Guatemala City, and San José, and would be making further stops in Barranquilla and Caracas before reaching Ciudad Bolívar. He'd chosen his stops based on Pan Am routes and Air Force bases, which had mostly worked out well for him. He'd knocked knees with a stout, foul-mouthed Pan Am pilot in Guatemala, and sweet-talked a blue jay out of a wide-eyed second lieutenant in Costa Rica.

Panama City was the place Guy had been looking forward to the most, however. First off, being "that way" wasn't illegal here, and Guy found it much easier to get a hard-on without the prospect of jail hanging over his head. Also, the U. S. of A. sent a steady stream of impressionable young men down to guard the Canal Zone. Prohibition had left their lips dry and thirsty and unprepared for a man with enough coin to buy them some leg-spreading libations.

After negotiating a place to stow his plane for the night, Guy decided to head into the city to find a bar. He ran into a Pan Am stewardess waiting for a taxi outside the airport. She had perfectly curled auburn hair and, according to her shiny metal lapel pin, was named Helen.

"You headed into town, mister?" Helen asked. She smelled of floral perfume and cigarette smoke.

"Planning on it. Do you know anywhere I can get a drink?"

"Depends. Are you just looking for a quick drink-a-vous or a full toot?" She spoke like a flapper, though she looked quite the opposite in her crisp blue uniform.

"Just a quick belt and a place to hang my hat. I'm flying out again in the morning."

"You're a flyboy?" She gave him a full scan with her heavily made-up green eyes

This dame is not subtle, Guy thought. He appreciated that, even if he wasn't interested. "I'm a pilot," he said.

Helen turned out to be quite a gas, and they ended up laughing the whole way into the city in a shared taxi.

"I'm heading to a dance with some friends," she confided. "Wanna come along?"

Guy shrugged. "Dancing isn't really my thing." Which was true—with women at least. There weren't a lot of joints where you could dance with a man out in the open.

"Too bad. Well, I know the perfect place for you. La Castaña. It's a fun mix of locals and foreigners. And they rent out the rooms upstairs." She winked at him. "I may be headed over there myself, later."

"I'll keep an eye out for you," Guy said, though he was sure he meant it in a different way than she took it.

Guy found La Castaña without a lot of searching. It was an open-air bar jutting off the side of a chalky white two-story stone building on a dirt road called Canal Boulevard, nowhere near the canal. A stone courtyard lead off to one side, and the tables had gas lanterns on them, though none were lit as the late afternoon sun was still bright.

The place was empty except for a man at the bar: a broad-shouldered fellow with a tawny cowboy hat perched atop his head. Underneath, his hair was blond as an Oklahoma wheat field. The closer Guy got, the more he liked what he saw. The blond wore a light blue shirt with a leather yoke that stretched beautifully across his back. He had the body of a decathlete, broad at the top, tapering into a slim waist. Then he tapered out again, his light pants stretching remarkably across his rear, pressing against the barstool so naturally that Guy imagined him an apple waiting to be plucked from the branch.

This was exactly how Guy liked to meet men. Foreign location, temporary stop, no chance of any awkward talk of "making this a thing." Tomorrow morning he would be back in the sky, free as a bird, but hopefully with some good memories of Panama City.

Guy leaned against the bar next to the blond. He meant to engage the man in conversation, but when the blond turned to him, Guy was struck mute by his eyes, blue as a prairie sky. He felt suddenly stupid, fawning over a man like some cow-eyed heroine, and said the first thing he could think of: "Now what beer is the least likely to make me vomit?"

Inwardly, he cringed, but he made sure to give the blond his most roguish smile.

"I'm afraid that even the least likely is still very likely to give you some trouble," the blond replied. His voice was principled, New England. He smiled, his dazzling square teeth framed by full lips the color of red earth. Guy quickly found his own mouth cotton dry.

"I'll take my chances, then. What are you having?" The blond's glass was half full but Guy wanted him to stick around for a while.

The blond held his stare and Guy felt his pulse quickening. "Atlas, best of a suspicious bunch. What's your name, friend?"

"Guy Harris. And yours?"

"It's McCracken. Call me Mac," the blond replied, tipping his hat.

The bartender, a short, round-faced, mustachioed man, was doing an excellent job of ignoring them. Guy wondered if he was being too forward. It might not be illegal to be "that way" in Panama, but it wasn't something any barkeep would encourage. When he managed to catch his eye, Guy made sure to use his most gravelly voice to say, "Two Atlas beers, please."

The man stood still, eyeing Guy but not moving. Stress crawled into Guy's belly.

"*Dos*," Mac said, and Guy turned to see that he was smiling even more broadly. "Forget where you are?"

"Surely the man knows what *two* means," Guy responded.

"It's a matter of respect." The statement could have been a rebuke, but Mac's warm eyes told him it wasn't.

The bartender got to work and Guy said to Mac, "I just flew in. That's my excuse." He maintained eye contact, looking to see if the other man was interested.

Mac arched an eyebrow. "Are you a pilot?"

"You could say that. I prefer 'soldier of fortune.'"

Mac smiled. "Well, Guy, it just so happens that I'm looking to hire a pilot. Or a soldier of fortune."

Guy had two rules: never make a business decision while drinking, and never bed a man he was doing business with. He had good reasons for both. Still, he was ready to break them. "I could be your man," Guy said, and let the words sit.

This time, both eyebrows went up, and that big, wide smile spread across his face.

Mac wanted more than a pilot.

"I need a pilot for six weeks. I'll pay five thousand— American, not Balboas—plus fuel."

That was a massive amount of kale, more than what the museum people were offering. The current state of his hard-on told Guy he would fly Mac anywhere for free just to get a look at what was in those trousers. Still, six weeks was quite a commitment. He didn't mix men and commitment, not any more. Surely they could just get this fuck out of their systems and then go about their business.

The bartender deposited their beers in front of them sloppily, warm foam spilling over the rims of the glasses.

"You've got yourself a deal," Guy said, throwing caution to the wind and settling on the stool beside him.

Mac raised his glass. "Tell you what, Guy. I'm renting a room here. Why don't we finish our beers, then discuss the details of our arrangement upstairs?"

Guy raised his glass and clinked it against Mac's, all the time thinking, *What the hell are you getting yourself into, Harris?*

The first thing Mac had noticed about Guy Harris was his left bicep. It was almost obscene, the bulbous muscle gently pushing against the tightening skin, hardening as Guy leaned against the bar. Every visible part of him was thick and strong. He was wearing white linen trousers, a thin red undershirt, and suspenders. He looked half-dressed and entirely inappropriate, but they were in a bar in Panama, not at one of Mac's mother's garden parties.

Then the dark-haired, dark-eyed man had said he was a pilot, a "soldier of fortune," and it was like Fate Herself had delivered Guy right to his barstool.

Ten years ago, Mac had taken his shiny Harvard biology degree and headed as far south as he could go. He was eager to find some way to give his mother the fortune she had always wanted, the one his father had always held just out of their reach. Mac had never worked with his hands before, but he knew animals and he knew there was real money to be made in South America, driving cattle up to the Canal Zone. On his trips back and forth over the past decade, he had secured just enough income to keep his mother in the expensive apartment his father had set her up in as his mistress. Now Mac had even bigger plans: he was going to make them a fortune.

But he had to be careful. Driving cattle in Central and South America was tricky business. There was always someone eager to stab you in the back. These weren't places to be aggressively pursuing men. So as a rule, he refused to show any carnal interest toward men, even men who ran their eyes over him like Guy had. It was just too dangerous. He had gotten a reminder just how dangerous last month. He'd been friendly, just friendly, with a lieutenant named Barry who would come by La Castaña every few days. One evening, Barry had had a few too many, and while practicing his elementary Spanish skills on a group of locals, he rested his hand on the thick thigh of a young man.

Observing, Mac had winced, but he figured Barry could play it off as a simple mistake.

No sooner had he thought that than the men had attacked Barry with startling ferocity. By the time Mac had reached him, he'd been beaten so badly he couldn't even open his swollen eyes. Behind the bar, Arturo hadn't said a word, just shook his head and checked the kegs.

And that story was tame compared to the reports Mac had heard about men who had been found dead in the canal, people laughing about it like it was what they deserved. He was not going to be one of those men.

Guy, however, made Mac feel comfortable on a deep level from the second they started talking. The thought made Mac feel a little disgusted with himself. He didn't need some man to make him feel safe. He was strong and worked hard at it.

Still, something about Guy made Mac want to take a risk, told him he would be okay if he did.

They finished their drinks and Mac looked at Guy levelly. He tried to sound smooth though his throat was tight. "Let's head upstairs, shall we?"

Helen stood in the entrance to the bar and shook her head. She'd been so taken with Mr. Guy Harris—that dashing pilot with the eyes like Costa Rican chocolate and the body of a Spartan—that she'd ditched her friends at the dance hall and come back to La Castaña to get in his pants. When she arrived, she found him making eyes at a corn-haired beauty, which didn't surprise her. That the corn-haired beauty was a man in a cowboy hat was a bit of an eye-opener, though.

Helen saw every sort in her line of work. *Maybe I can win him over*, she thought. *I've got charm enough.* She watched the men, looking for an opening. Neither one noticed her. Although she wasn't used to the feeling herself, Helen knew when Cupid's arrow had struck. She couldn't muster any surprise when the two men headed out through the courtyard to the rooms above the bar.

Arturo watched them go like a sad puppy. Helen's pride was sore, but she sure as hell wasn't going to let it show like that. She strode up to the bar and sat on the stool still warm from Guy Harris's perfect ass. *Probably as close as you'll ever get*, she told herself.

Arturo turned his puppy eyes to her. "Señorita?" he asked almost tonelessly.

"Kinda dead in here tonight, isn't it?"

"Sí."

"Too early to turn in."

The barkeeper gave a slow look at the courtyard entrance. "I would not go up there now."

"No?"

He looked at her. "No."

Helen sighed despite herself. "Cuba libre, partner, *por favor*," she said. "And heavy on the libre."

She took her drink to a table in the corner where she could keep an eye on the entrance and the courtyard. It was early yet. Maybe the place would fill up. It was worth waiting to see.

Mac's hand shook as he tried to fit the key into the lock. It had been years since he'd had sex with a man, and the prospect made him dizzy with lust and nerves. He also didn't like the way Arturo had eyed them from the bar. Although plenty of men retired to their rooms to smoke cigars and talk bull, the look worried Mac. He'd been renting at a very cheap rate in exchange for helping with odd jobs around the place. Mac had gotten a feeling about Arturo when he'd first met him, and so he performed his tasks in his undershirt. So long as he flirted with the older man and wore as little clothing as possible while carrying heavy things around in the heat, his room was practically free.

Now Mac wondered if Guy was playing the same game with him. If he paid Guy for piloting *and* slept with him, would he be paying Guy to sleep with him?

His mother would be horrified.

He was horrified.

But he was tired of playing everything safe.

He could feel Guy's heat radiating behind him as he opened the door. It was dark inside and would have been impossibly hot without a breeze. Mac hung his hat on a small rack to the left of the door before stepping over his suitcase to turn on the gas lantern in the corner.

The light filled the tiny room. It had a twin bed, its headboard bolted to the back wall. Small tables sat on either side, serving as a nightstand on the left and a bar on the right. Each table had a squat chair on which Mac had piled books and documents. Directly over the headboard was a map of Central America, the Caribbean, and the northern countries of South America.

Mac turned to face Guy, who leaned against the frame of

the door. The man was built like a baby grand. His muscles looked taut under his shirt, ready to pounce. His gaze rolled slowly up and down Mac's body. Mac could see that Guy had one thing on his mind, and it wasn't discussing their business arrangement.

Was he really ready for this? What was *this*, anyway? Mac had never been good at separating sex from feelings, and here he was trying to seduce a flyboy. Flyboys didn't really have a reputation for sticking around. Impulsively, he asked, "Do you want a drink? I've got a jug of boiled water, or I could pour you something stronger."

Guy smiled. "Stronger would be great."

Maybe I just need some liquid courage, Mac thought. If Guy's forward approach was anything to go by, the pilot was experienced in these matters. Mac was not.

He moved directly to his "bar." He pulled two glasses from the shelf below and poured two fingers from a brown bottle into each glass. He held a glass out to Guy, who finally left the doorframe and met him halfway at the foot of the bed.

"Here's your cocktail, flyboy," Mac said.

Guy surveyed the glass in the dim light. "What's on the menu?" he asked.

Mac gulped. He hoped Guy didn't think he was slowing things down because he wasn't interested. He was just worried he would faint or throw up—or both—if Guy did so much as touch him. "Cane spirits. Bootleg back at home but less than a clam for a whole case here."

Guy gave it a sniff and winced. "How about a toast? Here's mud in your eye."

Mac raised his glass to meet Guy's, and with both their gazes and glasses touching Mac was sure that Guy was going to kiss him. Then Guy took a sip of his drink, gagged, and coughed out a mist, coating Mac's face.

"Holy hell, man, that stuff is dangerous!"

Mac wiped his face with his rolled up sleeve and clapped Guy on the back. "Here, sit down, old boy." Mac eased Guy onto the foot of the bed, where his coughing turned into laughter.

Mac felt at ease touching Guy, which surprised him as he had never felt comfortable touching any man. He was always afraid his hand would move too far, that it would reveal some interest he wouldn't be able to hide.

Guy said, "Okay, Mac, you'd better explain this job to me before I get distracted."

The word *distracted* set McCracken's heart hammering. "Sure," he croaked. "How about I show you on the map?" He pointed to the head of the bed.

"After you."

Mac removed his shoes and crawled to the top of the bed, taking a gulp of his drink before setting it on the table and raising himself on his knees. He leaned one hand on the wall and used the other to point, his back to Guy.

He pointed to Panama City. "We're here, see?"

"I see."

Mac looked over his shoulder and saw that Guy was certainly not looking at the map.

Emboldened, Mac said, "Come closer so you can see what I'm talking about."

Mac turned back to the map and heard two thunks as Guy's shoes hit the floor. He felt Guy crawl onto the bed, stopping directly behind him, also on his knees. He placed his hands on the wall on either side of the map, caging Mac in. Guy had the smell of a man who worked with machines, that light scent of gasoline and oil, but beneath those base notes, hints of cinnamon, sandalwood, and sweat.

"Okay," Guy said. "Show me."

Mac struggled to remember what he'd been talking about. He turned his focus to the map. "So, we head east. First we need to get here." He pointed to the bottom part of Venezuela, which stuck out like the foot of a clam. "San Carlos de Rio Negro."

"Mmm-hmm. Keep going," Guy whispered, his breath hot on Mac's neck.

"From there we need to fly north over the Amazon Jungle, toward Angostura. Though this map is outdated; it's called Ciudad Bolívar now. We'll stop here, at the Gran

Sábana," he said, pointing to a big empty stretch in the southeast corner of Venezuela.

"I was headed that way anyways," Guy said and moved his hands from the wall to Mac's hips.

Mac's lust was turning his stomach. He wondered if he had bitten off more than he could chew.

The bar was filling up with a mixture of locals and foreigners, just like she said it would. Helen's second Cuba libre had disappeared a bit too quickly, though, so she got out her nail file and tended to a little personal vanity. She didn't notice when the man approached.

"A beautiful woman should not drink alone."

Helen looked up. The man was presentable enough, trim mustache and clean hair, surprising hazel eyes, and his English was pretty good. But there was a teetering to his stance that told her La Castaña was not his first stop tonight. "How kind of you to notice, Señor, but I am waiting for someone."

The man looked around, mostly at a table of other locals, who were all eyeing him with wolfish grins. He turned back to her. "Why wait?"

Because you're too drunk and I'm not drunk enough, she thought. She gave him her best Pan Am smile. "I already have plans for the evening, thank you."

The man leaned on the table, supporting himself with his knuckles. "Maybe plans can change, no?"

She felt sorry for him. A man with so many assets and yet a complete lack of polish. "No," she said, her smile almost sympathetic as she twirled the nail file in her fingers.

The gesture was lost on her admirer but not on Arturo. He was at her table in an instant. "Is there a problem?" he asked, his eyes hard as anthracite.

"Just the usual, Arturo." She looked apologetically at the barkeeper. "We have a customer here who doesn't seem to know the house rules."

"Let me take care of this, Señorita."

"Why?" the man demanded, hauling himself upright. "Is she some great lady?"

Helen admired the way Arturo handled it. Though shorter, his intensity of focus gave him the upper hand. He called the man *amigo* and led him away firmly by the arm and spoke to him in a low voice. Helen looked down and resumed her filing to give them some privacy. When she looked up again, the drunk glanced her way, wiped his mouth, and with a short nod returned to his friends.

She thanked Arturo with a smile and he returned it with a look of smug satisfaction. Then some other emotion crossed his face, darkening it. He turned and walked to the table where the locals had gathered and said a few words she could not hear. Then without looking back he left through the courtyard. *What's that* loro viejo *up to now?* she wondered. The evening was definitely getting interesting.

Mac felt Guy's knees move between his legs, pushing them gently wider. He felt pinned and exposed. Mac was roughly the same size as Guy, just a bit thinner, but in this position he felt like he had relinquished power. He didn't want to be Guy's moll.

Guy moved his hands up, pressing his fingers into Mac's hard abdomen. "So strong," he said into Mac's neck. He worked his hands up to Mac's chest and started slowly undoing the top button of his shirt.

Mac tried to regain control by outlining the journey, hoping it would distract Guy from his inexperience. "What we're looking for is northeast of the rainforest but south of Ciudad Bolívar."

Guy moved to the second button. "And what is it we're looking for?"

"Cattle. I'm a cowboy. They're paying a pretty penny for outsiders to come down and drive cattle back up to the Canal Zone."

Guy pushed his erection against Mac's backside while starting on the third button. It felt huge and McCracken felt nervous and even *more* aroused, which he hadn't known was possible.

"You don't have to go all the way to Venezuela to find a bull."

Mac laughed, a short sharp bark.

Guy buried his head in Mac's shoulder. "Okay, that was bad. Let me try again. How about, why are you willing to pay so much for *this* bull?" He pushed his erection against him again.

Mac went silent. Guy really *was* doing this for the money.

As if he'd read his mind, Guy stopped thrusting. "Not funny?"

The seduction had gone on long enough. It was time to get down to business. "I don't want to pay for *this* bull," Mac said, pushing his ass against Guy. "I'm *paying* you to be my pilot. I want *you* for free."

Guy finished the third button. Mac's chest was now exposed. "I'm not doing this because you're paying me," he said firmly in his ear. "I'm doing this because you're gorgeous." He flicked Mac's nipples.

"Holy shit!" Mac shuddered, his mind blanking. Who knew *that* felt like *that*?

After several more moments of that delightful, mysterious stroking, which left him frenzied, Guy moved his hands down to Mac's trousers. Unlike his languid pace with the shirt buttons, he undid the clips lightning fast. "Lift up," he said, and when Mac did he swiftly pulled them past his ankles and tossed them to the floor. Mac thought that he must look absurd, kneeling there in his Jockeys, ass in the air, chest bursting out of his shirt, garters and socks still on.

Guy brought his right hand up and grabbed Mac's chin, pulling it firmly to the right. He aligned their faces and planted a kiss on Mac's lips. The kiss told him, sure as a map, exactly what Guy planned on doing with him.

The room shook suddenly with a pounding on the door.

"Señor McCracken! Señor McCracken!" a voice called. "I need your help!"

It was Arturo. Mac jerked halfway off the bed. Guy held him firmly with one hand, and with the other put a finger to his lips, smiling. Mac shook his head and mouthed, *I have to go.* Guy frowned and released him.

Mac opened the door a crack, being careful to shield most of his undressed state. "Arturo, what in the name of God—"

"The water in *los baños*, señor," Arturo said. "It must be changed."

Mac saw him rake his eyes over his open shirt. He retreated behind the door. "What, now?"

"*Sí*, at once. It is most important."

Arturo's eyes glittered with a hardness Mac had not seen before. "Okay. Give me a minute."

"At once, Señor."

"Okay, okay. I'm coming."

Arturo stared him briefly in the face, then turned and left.

Mac closed the door and started pulling on his pants.

"You're not really leaving, are you?" Guy asked. He was leaning back on the mattress, one arm resting behind his head, that perfect bicep waiting for him.

"I have to. He lets me stay here if I help out."

Guy's face hardened instantly. "If you're working for your rent, how can you afford to pay me so much coin?"

"That's why I can pay you so much coin, flyboy. Look, this won't take long. I want to continue our . . . discussion. Stick around."

Guy shrugged. "Maybe I will, maybe I won't."

Mac wanted this man. But he needed this cattle drive more, and that depended on his agreement with Arturo. He fished his key out of his pocket and tossed it to Guy. "If you don't stay, lock up. Leave the key with the barkeep." He shut the door behind him, unsure if he was more terrified that Guy would be gone when he got back or still there in his bed.

The gas lanterns were lit when Guy returned to the bar. Their golden light combined with the warm, salty air and the laughter of the patrons to give the place a festive atmosphere. *Panama must be quite the melting pot*, Guy thought looking over the crowd. The men came in every color, from blue black to deep brown, and all the way up the delicious spectrum. Guy didn't discriminate. If a stranger had a cock and a nice smile, chances are he'd be interested.

But tonight he found something slightly wrong with each of them. He looked at one local with broad shoulders and a shaved head. *His teeth are too big*, Guy thought.

He glanced at another, obviously not from Panama with creamy skin and red hair. *Too many freckles*, Guy thought.

He looked at a group of guys at a table. He surveyed them all, particularly their backsides, and found them lacking.

He knew where this sudden picky streak was coming from. There was only one ass he wanted to think about now. He had looked for Mac as he passed through the courtyard, but there was no sign of him. He cursed. *Never make a business decision while drinking, and never bed a man you're in business with*, he repeated to himself. He had his rules for a reason. Up in Mac's room, he'd nearly broken both. Now he worried the thrill he'd gotten upstairs was curdling into something heartbreaking. He needed a drink.

He sat at the bar and looked at Arturo, who eyed him with disdain. He was sure there was jealousy there, too, something Mac was using to his advantage. He waved him over. "*Hola,*" Guy said when he stopped in front of him.

Arturo's face was a challenge. A drop of sweat dripped from the bottom of his mustache.

"That's right, isn't it? *Hola?*"

Arturo grimaced. *"Que quieres?"*

Guy's Spanish was basic. He'd learned enough growing up in Oklahoma to communicate with the farmhands, and heard if you ordered something *en fuego* it would be extra strong. He wasn't sure what to order *en fuego* here, though. Considering the devilish stuff Mac had poured into his glass, he decided on something he could be sure of. "Atlas, *por favor.*"

Arturo looked unimpressed but turned to the tap.

Guy felt a squeeze on his shoulder and his heart fluttered. Despite himself, he smiled. He turned, expecting to see Mac's blue eyes staring into his. Instead, it was a man with light brown skin and hazel eyes, slightly shorter than Guy, and built like a pit bull. He was angry.

"What were you looking at, friend?" The man asked, his English slow and over-enunciated. His eyes alternated between staring at him and flicking back to a table of men, the ones whose butts Guy had found lacking. *Uh oh*, Guy thought.

He squared his shoulders. He knew the quickest way to be attacked would be to show fear. He wasn't afraid of this man, but he didn't think he could fight him and the men from his table as well. Guy was without backup unless Arturo decided to help, which he doubted. He stood up. "I'm not sure what you mean, friend," he said, refusing to break eye contact.

"You were checking us out, *puto.*"

Guy knew very well what *puto* meant. He squinted his eyes and took a step forward. "I'm sorry, *friend*, I don't know what you mean. Maybe you'd like to explain it to me."

The other man looked fearful for a moment, but then glanced back at his friends. They were no longer sitting. That seemed to bolster his confidence. He turned back. "You want us."

Guy figured he might outrun these idiots, but his pride would never let him do that. He decided that it was time to go down fighting. How much damage could he do this guy before his friends from across the room joined in? Probably not enough, but it would feel pretty good. He flexed his hands, squeezing them into fists.

The man's eyebrows went up. He looked scared briefly, but once more glanced at his approaching posse and gained confidence. He took a final step toward Guy. He was either about to sneer a final taunt or spit in his face when a mellifluous voice called out behind him.

"Guy, darling! Where the hell have you been?"

Helen had seen Guy re-enter the bar. *Huh,* she thought, *that was quick, even for a flyboy.* She shook her head as he stared openly at the other men, wondering if he had some kind of death wish. He turned his back to the room and ordered a drink. With rising alarm, she watched as one of the men walked over to Guy and the others got to their feet. She looked at Arturo, wondering if he would intervene. The look on his face told her all she needed to know. He was enjoying this. She'd have to handle this one herself.

She opened her compact and took a quick look in the mirror, pleased to see a slightly buzzed but still beautiful gal with perfectly styled auburn hair staring back. She rose to her feet, calling out, "Guy, darling! Where the hell have you been?" and pretended to stumble over, walking right between Guy and the local.

She put her hands on Guy's shoulders, blocking him from his would-be assailant. She looked into those beautiful brown eyes and made sure he recognized her. She grabbed his head with both hands and planted a kiss right on his startled lips.

Then she slapped him across the face.

It felt good.

"That's for making your sheba wait," she said. Then she leaned in and murmured in a sultry voice loud enough for the men behind her to hear, "And this is for finally showing up," and she wrapped him tightly in her arms and kissed him again. Guy stood there, frozen. Helen had the feeling that Guy's mouth hadn't touched a woman's in a while. She knew she tasted of cigarettes and sweet liquor, while his mouth had a distinctly *male* taste that turned her on more than it should. She whispered in his ear, "Kiss me back, you sap. Like you mean it." She winked and went in for another. This time, he kissed back, giving it his best show. Then she pushed him away. "Now, get me a drink!"

She turned to face the brute and his friends and smiled, calling over her shoulder at Guy, "Cuba isn't going to free itself, you know."

"This is the one you wait for?" the man asked, frowning.

"None other. He's my sheik and I'm his sheba."

The man snorted. "Lady, your sheik's a faggot," he said.

Helen threw her head back and laughed. She knew she had an excellent laugh. She'd practiced.

"My Guy? A three-letter man? Now I *know* you're mistaken! And I'm never wrong about these things." She turned to the bar. "Am I, Arturo?"

The men could not see the look she gave him. His face did not move a muscle. "No, Señorita," he said.

"There, you see?" she said, turning back to the man. She swatted him on the shoulder just hard enough to make sure he felt her perfectly-manicured nails.

The man was rattled. "But he was staring at us!"

She smiled flirtatiously. "Well, who wouldn't keep an eye on a handsome group like you? With all these strapping young bulls down here, Guy's a little self-conscious." She winked and held out her pinkie. "You know, just a little."

The man grinned. "Then why are you with him and not one of us?"

Helen laughed and put a hand on her hip. "You can't hear it, can you? That's Oklahoma oil in his voice, *chicos*." She leaned forward and told them in a stage whisper, "He's rich as a sultan! Even owns his own plane. Watch, I'll show you." She called back to Guy, who was still fetching her Cuba libre. "Lover, a round of tequila for all of these fine young men!"

She was going to make him empty his wallet for this. He deserved it, she was that good. At this rate, they'd be carrying Guy around on their shoulders by the end of the night.

Mac stepped into the bathing stalls and wrinkled his nose. Moonlight illuminated the small roofless space, but the stagnant water made it far from romantic. He could hear voices on the other side of the building where the bar was filling up with the nightly crowd. He'd have been part of that crowd if Guy hadn't shown up, and he'd be with Guy right now if Arturo hadn't shown up.

Arturo was good about boiling up water for drinking and bathing each day. The safe water filled the cisterns above the showers, and a trough caught the run-off to keep it from muddying the courtyard. It was Mac's job to empty the trough and fill the cisterns. He'd done it already once today.

Still, Arturo had told him to empty the waste water and fill all the cisterns again.

He pulled the heavy trough out of the stalls and over to the back of the property. The water would get dumped over the fence, where it ran into an open gutter. The trough was too heavy to lift, so Mac used a bucket to dip out the gray water, trying not to think too much about what was in it, and pour it over the fence. As Mac hauled the last bucket up to the fence, he heard a woman's voice pierce the air. He'd been aware of a low rumbling tension coming from the bar. Remembering Barry, he emptied the bucket quickly and went to the courtyard entrance and looked in.

Mac searched for Guy and was surprised to find him in the arms of a beautiful woman, a Pan Am girl from the looks of her, locked in a kiss. Every hair on his body raised electrically as he watched the flyboy put his moves on the stewardess. Was she nibbling his ear or whispering into it? Once more Guy kissed her indulgently. Mac's face burned and he turned away.

What was Guy doing with that dame? His mind churned as he started refilling the cisterns with fresh water. Mac was certain Guy was interested in him. Or had been. He hadn't promised to be there when he got back. *Flyboys aren't known for sticking around*, he reminded himself. Maybe Guy was one of those with attraction to both sexes. Maybe it was first come, first served with him. Mac thought again how safe and comfortable Guy had made him feel. That wasn't all bull, was it? Guy hadn't been playing with him, had he?

Mac filled the bucket for the last cistern, his muscles straining. But as he hauled it up to dump into the tank, a cheer went up from the bar. It startled him, turning his head and tipping him off balance. His grip slipped and the bucket tumbled down his arm, dumping its contents right onto his face and torso.

Mac gasped. He was soaking wet. He looked down and saw that his thin clothing was now basically translucent. He needed to go back to his room and change before anyone saw him like this. He crossed the courtyard and hurried up the stairs to the balcony outside the rooms, but when he reached his door, he stopped. He'd be furious if Guy had left the room unlocked, but screwed if he hadn't. Hoping against hope, he tried the latch. No dice. And now he was without a key to his room, dressed in clothes that clung to and highlighted every detail underneath. He couldn't go into the bar like this, but he couldn't think of any other way to get to Guy or Arturo, the only people who had a key.

Guy was wondering how he was going to get the Cuba libre and tray of tequilas to Helen and the "young bulls" when he

saw her turn to him and hold up a finger. The locals had settled back at their table. She winked at them and said, "Watch
and learn boys. This is how a professional delivers a drink."

With that, she strutted back to the bar with her best air-
craft-aisle-shuffle, her bombastic hip movements working on
the men. When she reached Guy, she gave him a kiss on the
cheek, grabbed her Cuba libre with one hand and the tray
with the other, and sashayed back with that same aggressive
wiggle, holding the tray above her head with ease. She placed
the tray on their table and held her glass high, saying with a
light-hearted lilt:

> *"If wishing damns us, you and I*
> *Are damned to all our hearts' content;*
> *Come then, at least we may enjoy*
> *Some pleasure for our punishment."*

The whole bar cheered. The locals sipped their tequilas
and Helen curtsied to the men, blew a kiss, and sauntered
back to Guy. She gave him a bright smile and a wink on her
way across the bar.

He slipped an arm around her waist, genuinely impressed.
"How did you do that? They fell in love with you in an instant."

She pulled away slightly. "That's it? Not even a thank
you?"

Guy felt his cheeks redden. "I'm sorry. I—"

She waved her Cuba libre at him. "Skip it. Let's go over there where we can talk."

She led him to a corner table and sat, Guy noted, facing the room. He sat opposite. *This woman is no flapper*, he thought. "Seriously, though, how did you do it?" he asked again.

"Darling, that's what I do for a living. Make silly men fall in love with me for a little while." She smiled wanly. "At least I'm not trapped in an aircraft with this lot."

"The way you move, you could be a film star."

Helen laughed whole-heartedly. "Why would I do something like that? Being a Pan Am girl is better than being a film star. We get to travel the world, meet exciting people, dress up every day. Everywhere we go people recognize us. I haven't bought myself a drink in years." She lowered her voice. "Though I must say I usually don't have to work *this* hard for it, particularly with no chance of a *tip*, if you catch my drift."

Guy looked down and blushed again. "Thank you," he said quietly. He looked up. "So, how did you know? Am I giving off vibes?"

She took a sip of her cocktail and looked him square in the eye. "I'm going to tell you something, even though I've got to swallow my pride to do it." She took another, deeper drink. "My girlfriends were *horribly* dull tonight, so I thought 'screw it,' and jumped back in a cab to come find you. I got here and saw you talking to that ab-so-*lute*-ly gorgeous blond. Other men would have seen me, a single girl standing at the entrance to a bar. But neither of you even glanced my way. I know a man in love when I see one."

Guy was shocked. "He was looking at me like a man in love?"

She half-smiled and shook her head. "I don't know, you sod. I wasn't looking at him. I'm talking about you."

He stared at her. Then he swallowed and said, "It's just supposed to be a business arrangement."

Helen raised an eyebrow. "He didn't look like the sort, but I guess that makes him good at it." She raised her glass in salute.

"No! Not *that* kind of business!" he hissed. "He needs an aviator for a job. But I don't mix business and pleasure. Not usually. And I'm thinking I shouldn't this time either. We were interrupted. Maybe it's a sign."

Helen smirked. "Sure it is, Guy." She downed her drink. "How about a refill? If we're going to keep lying to ourselves, we might as well get bent while we're at it."

Mac knew his best bet would be to go down to the courtyard and stand in the light that spilled from the bar. Hopefully he could catch Arturo's eye or Guy's before too many patrons took notice.

As he stood in the dim light, he could see Guy's broad shoulders seated at a table, but his back was to him. He and the auburn-haired woman were in deep conversation, her face lighting up with laughter. Sadness hit Mac like he had walked into a brick wall. Of course. Guy was one of those who would always adapt, always fit in, act *normal,* if that's what you wanted to call it. This wasn't just a different sort of attraction, this was a different Guy.

Arturo spotted him from behind the bar, his bushy eyebrows shooting straight up. He walked briskly out to him. "What the hell are you doing, man?" he demanded.

Tearing his eyes from Guy, Mac said simply. "Locked out. Do you have another key?"

Arturo stepped back and looked Mac up and down. With the wet clothing clinging to his body, Mac knew he was seeing things he hadn't seen before. "That key was expensive," Arturo said. "It'll cost you."

Mac cringed. It wasn't just the look; he was used to that from Arturo by now. But tonight, after Guy had made him feel wanted for who he was, the leering felt different. He felt exposed and dirty.

One of the men inside shouted something in Spanish. Arturo's interaction with Mac was drawing attention. Mac looked to see if Guy noticed the commotion, and for a moment it looked like he would turn his way.

His hope vanished when the Pan Am girl placed her hand on Guy's arm. Guy froze, not even able to look at him.

Something inside Mac shifted. He looked at Arturo again. Men like him didn't know how to love. Shame and pride prevented them from pursuing affection honestly. They had to cast it as payment or a bribe. Arturo's way of looking at him wasn't demeaning, it was pathetic.

"Give me the key," he growled.

The barkeeper's eyes went wide. He pulled a key off his ring and handed it to him.

"Thanks," he rumbled and hurried back to his room.

Someone shouted something in Spanish and Helen looked up. It became suddenly a lot easier to understand why Guy had fallen for the blond when she saw him standing there in his wet clothing. "Wowzers," she breathed.

Guy started to turn around. "Unh-uhn," she said, putting a hand on his arm.

"Is it—?"

"Yep, but now is not the time for heroics. Let Arturo handle it." She released his arm and he stayed put. He was rigid with tension. She pulled out a cigarette. "Got a light?"

He reached slowly for his pocket. "If he's in trouble—"

"Listen, flyboy, I didn't save the furniture from being

212

busted up by some *macho Americano* display only to have it busted up by *two* macho Americanos. Relax."

He stretched out his match for her cigarette. His hand trembled. She glanced at the doorway again. "There, see? All taken care of. He's gone."

The air seemed to go out of her companion. He slumped in his chair and wouldn't look at her. She took a deep drag on her cigarette and shook her head sadly. "Guy Harris. If there is one thing I've learned in my profession it's that a love affair doesn't need to be long to be good and it doesn't need to be good to be long."

Guy still wouldn't look up but she knew he was listening.

"But any love affair deserves to be seen through to its natural end. And you and that man have more miles to fly before you get there."

Guy looked up and she could see the conflict play across his face. She leaned forward and touched his cheek.

"I'm a Pan Am girl. I might not know what it's like to be you, but I do know what it's like to want to run from one place to the next without taking anything with you but yourself. I love it because I love being lonely," she said.

Guy laughed softly.

"I mean it. Being lonely keeps me in constant company. But you and I aren't the same, Harris. You're not meant to be flying solo."

"Lady, you're a sap," he said.

"It's the tequila," she said, crushing out her cigarette. "The coast is clear now, I think. Time for us to go." She stood up.

Guy rose, a puzzled look on his face. "Go where?"

"Where do you think?" She held out her arm.

His eyes widened. "You have a room here?"

She chuckled. "You really are thick, aren't you? Too bad I'll never find out just how thick." She slipped her arm into his. "Come on, lover, let's give the locals a show."

For the second time that evening, Guy found himself climbing the stairs to the rooms above the bar. He and Helen were halfway up when Arturo caught up with them.

"Señor," he said. "Señor, I'm sorry, but the tab."

Helen turned and looked down at him. "I've changed my mind," she said. "It's on the house."

Arturo opened his mouth but nothing came out. He closed it, nodded, and hurried back to the bar.

Guy climbed the rest of the stairs, questions whirling in his head. When they got to the top, he asked the only one he could. "Who are you?"

She smiled and opened her purse. "Your Spanish isn't really very good, is it?"

He shook his head. "No, not really."

"But your friend's is. He stays here a lot, I'm told." She pulled out a key and disengaged his arm. "Ask him what *la castaña* means." She gave him a wink and walked on down the balcony to her room.

He turned and realized they had stopped outside Mac's room. He hesitated for a moment, then tapped lightly.

"Arturo, I'll return the key tomorrow. *Mañana!*"

"It's Guy."

After a moment, the door creaked open.

The look on Mac's face was a mix of caution and surprise. He was wearing only a towel, which Guy found to be more than a little distracting.

"Get dumped by the stewardess?" he asked. He wasn't smiling.

"In a way," Guy said. He held his breath.

Mac hesitated, then stepped aside to let him in.

Mac sat on the bed and motioned him to sit on one of the small chairs. This put him at eye level with Mac's thighs, which were pressed tightly together. He glanced up to meet his eyes, but on the way he saw that Mac's nipples were hard despite the heat. He remembered flicking them earlier, which had nearly sent the cowboy into convulsions. "I want to pick up where we left off," he said.

Mac's legs relaxed a bit and it was all Guy could do not to shove his face right up under that towel.

"Do you mean business or pleasure?" Mac asked.

"Yes. I mean no. I mean both."

Mac looked at him. "Well, that pretty much covers it."

"I don't mix business and pleasure," Guy blurted out.

Mac snorted sarcastically.

"I mean, as a rule. For a reason. And I don't do relationships. Again, for a reason."

Mac straightened up, his thighs clenched together.

Guy continued before he lost his nerve. "I took a fellow on an trip once. An oil guy. Wanted to do some measurements out in the Gulf of Mexico, needed me to do some flyovers. I was young and he was a looker. Anyway, long story short, I got in his pants, and he convinced me to let him pay me after the job was done. I flew him all over, and he kept me satisfied the whole time. Told me things no man has ever told me. I trusted him. Right near the end of our planned timetable, we took a detour to Cuba. Romantic. We got drunk, fucked, and when I woke up in the morning my plane had been sold out from under me and the bastard was gone."

Guy had never told anyone about it, and it was a relief to have it off of his chest until he realized that Mac hadn't responded.

"So, does this mean you just want to keep this as business?" Mac asked.

"No," Guy said. His eyes wandered down, wishing Mac would open his legs again. "But I don't want to mess everything up. Like I said, I've got rules for a reason."

Mac stood up. His legs shifted beneath the towel, and an impressive—and hard—manhood shook with the movement. He squeezed between Guy and the wall, his butt nearly hitting Guy in the face. He busied himself at the bar, and when he turned around he held two small glasses of that poison he'd served earlier.

"You know, flyboy, I drove myself crazy thinking of you as some experienced lothario, and me as some innocent you were going to prey on," Mac said.

"I was looking forward to the preying," Guy admitted.

"Well, let's stop torturing ourselves. Our 'piloting' arrangement doesn't begin until tomorrow. For now, I'd like to share a toast with a very handsome 'soldier of fortune.'"

Guy laughed as Mac handed him the drink. "How about something more elegant than 'Here's mud in your eye'?" He stood up.

"If wishing damns us, you and I

Are damned to all our hearts' content."

"Hey, I know that one," Mac said, continuing:

"Come then, at least we may enjoy

Some pleasure for our punishment."

Guy laughed and downed a slug, this time without coughing it up. He wiped his chin and shook his head. "You know it too, huh? Where'd you hear it?"

Mac shrugged. "Around. Here, I guess. At La Castaña." He

sat down on the bed, his legs spread resplendently as he took a drink.

Guy stared. He knew he'd have to ask his question before he forgot his own name. "So, what does it mean, *la castaña*?"

"Umm," Mac took a sip. "*Castaño* is chestnut, a chestnut tree. *La castaña* would be . . . a chestnut itself, I guess."

"Huh."

"Or chestnut-colored."

A grin spread across Guy's face. "Or auburn."

"Sure." Mac lifted his glass, leaning against the headboard and opening his legs further. "To La Castaña."

With his left hand, Guy began unbuckling his belt. With his right he held up his glass. "I'll drink to that."

OLIVE URCHIN

≳ 1 ≲
Detailing the arrival of Olive Urchin

At the tippity-top of Hong Kong Island, above the tree line of wealth that prevents the common folk from setting down roots in its soil, there is one thing that all homes large and small contain: a maid; and one such maid will be the focus of this tale that I have long wanted to tell.

Olive came to live with my family on my tenth birthday. I am embarrassed to admit that in many ways I thought of her as my birthday present. My parents had fired our previous maid Ginger just a week before. Ginger had been with us for nearly the entire time we had lived in Hong Kong, almost two years, and I missed her terribly. Following my mother around to all of her appointments, massages, and teas was exhausting.

The day before my birthday, I overheard my mother on the phone. It was impossible not to overhear phone conversations in our apartment. Though we lived in the Mid-Levels, "almost the best part of Hong Kong," according to my mother, our apartment on Conduit Road was about a fourth of the size of the house we'd had in Boston. I could tell my mother was talking about a maid because her and her friends didn't use names when she talked about Ginger or other people's maids. Only pronouns.

"Okay, but is she Malaysian? I just can't handle Malaysians. They can't take directions. So disrespectful." Ginger had been from Kuala Lumpur.

"Oh. Vietnamese? You know, I just don't know. My father served in Vietnam. You *know* what they did to Americans there, don't you? Those people just don't value life the same way we do."

"Oh, she's that young? Her parents weren't even in the war? How old is she?"

"Yes, I've seen her picture. She's light-skinned for a maid, which is good. Oh, that's why you called her Olive? Because of her olive skin? I'm not sure I'd call it olive, but I see what you're doing there. I was so sick of people staring at Ginger with my kids, like I'd let some street person kidnap them. And she's not too pretty, which is good. Ha!"

My mother's laugh was more of a squawk than a laugh. It served as punctuation. She never laughed in the middle of a sentence, only to end it.

"Okay, well, you owe us after how Ginger worked out."

"Five thousand a month? That's five hundred US. Does everyone pay that much?"

"Okay, fine. We'll do forty-five hundred. That's my limit. You know, we're giving her a roof over her head, too. Free rent. You know?"

"Okay, bring her by tomorrow. Dickey will be distracted by the party and Barney's going to drop the girls off at the Corneys' house for the day."

"Why are you telling me that? I know about Sundays off."

"Ginger said that? Ginger is a lying thief and that's why she's back in Malaysia. I always gave her Sundays off. You ask these people to do one little thing. You know how it is."

My mother hung up and I heard her in the kitchen, fiddling with the dishwasher. A few turns and cranks and then the click-clack of heels across the tiled floor after she gave up.

A new maid. I was so excited. A new friend. She would take me to school, watch me during the day, make my meals, and take me to my friends' houses. If I had made any friends. I'd spent all of my time with Ginger. She and I would walk the dog together every evening. Actually we'd walk the quarter mile up the road to the walking path that led to the top of Victoria Peak and sit on a bench. Ginger would send text messages and I'd play on my Nintendo DS while our Samoyed, Fledermaus, sniffed around the ferns.

I woke up late the morning of my birthday. It was July and school was out for the summer. It was cold, our apartment at its usual sixty-eight degrees, despite the temperature outside approaching a hundred. In our time in Hong Kong I had discovered it to be the coldest city I had ever visited. Its natural temperatures soared high, but every home, shop, school, and taxi, and subway had its air conditioning set to frigid temperatures. Boston, in my memory, was like the center of some nostalgic sun.

I wandered towards the kitchen, hoping to get to the living room unnoticed, where I could turn on my Playstation 2 and get my headphones on before my mother noticed. I rounded the corner into the kitchen and found my mother dramatically turning the knobs of the coffee maker, demonstrating for the girl standing next to her.

"Dicky! Happy Birthday, my love!" my mother squealed when she saw me, and click-clacked across the kitchen to wrap me in her arms. She smelled like her dress-up perfume, and the fabric of her glittery top scraped against my cheek as she hugged me.

She gestured to the girl, who reminded me more of the older boys at my school than of a girl. She was tall for an Asian girl. She was wearing brand new sneakers, which made her a little taller, but not nearly as much as my mother's heels made her. Her face was handsome, plain and angled like a tortured video game hero's. Her hair was cut short, curling around her ears, each of which had a greenish stone poking out of the lobe. She was wearing a short-sleeved, blue button-down shirt that fit her well across her broad shoulders but at the chest and waist looked about three times too big. It had a patch on it that said "Mrs. Mann's Maids" in fancy cursive. Her arm muscles were taut and round and I wondered if she played sports at school. Her black skirt was also too big, held on by a thin gold belt that she kept adjusting, like something itchy on a Halloween costume.

Her presence made my mother, with her big lips and big boobs and perfect makeup, look even prettier. "Darling, this is our new domestic helper, Olive. Say hello to Olive."

"Is Olive your real name?" I asked her. Ginger's real name had been Batrysia, and my mother had yelled at her for telling me. I figured I would get it out of the way early this time.

My mother's eyes and lips opened in her fake surprised look, all perfect "O" shapes.

"Dicky, that is very rude. Olive is the name she has chosen to use here and we will respect her decision."

"Ginger said you made her use a different name," I pointed out.

"Richard, that is enough! It is easier for *them* if we let them choose a new name for themselves."

She turned away from me then.

"Olive, you'll need to take Fledermaus for three walks a day. Take Dicky with you if he's around, he needs the exercise." She tossed a look back in my direction, challenging me to talk back. "There are poo bags in the front closet. You'll also need to take a water bottle with you to clean the sidewalk off with if he piddles."

She continued showing Olive things in the kitchen. I grabbed a pop tart and set myself up on the couch, ready for a day of video games. I was going to put my headphones on, but I found myself curious as to what my mother would say to Olive, and eager to hear if Olive would say anything in return. There was something exciting about Olive. She was like a mixture between a boy and a girl. And her face was completely blank. Everyone my mother knew had huge reactions to everything. They said "Oh my God" to everything my mother said. And my father was always either laughing or pretending to listen while doing something else. Olive's face was present and emotionless.

Eventually my mother led Olive through the living room, continuing her list of instructions and explanations. "My husband, Barney—call him Mr. Bumble—often works late, so you'll have to cook meals that can be easily reheated. And I work from home—I design handbags—so you can reach me in case of an emergency, but I don't like to be disturbed during office hours."

I rarely saw my mother in her office, what could have been the largest bedroom in the house but instead held her "mood boards" and the two handbags that she had made and not thrown into the trash somewhere in the process.

"And this," my mother told the still-blank-faced Olive while opening a door on the other side of the living room, "is your room."

Olive's room was also the laundry room, and had a single bed, a miniature refrigerator, and a nightstand in addition to the washer and dryer and ironing board that folded out from the wall. It had white tile floors and one small, circular window that faced the side of the building next door. It was the smallest room in the apartment, the next smallest being the guest bathroom.

After they'd done the rounds, my mother returned to the living room with Olive in tow, and sighed heavily, like she'd just finished a particularly difficult task. "Okay Olive, that's all for now. I've left a list of important rules, numbers, recipes, and things like that in your nightstand, so have a look at that. You'll need to clean things up before Dicky's party this evening, which starts at six, and make sure he's showered and dressed in the outfit I left on his bed. I've got to get to my massage, so if you try to call and I don't pick up you'll know why. The girls are at the Corneys' house. They have your cell number so make sure you have it on you. You can meet the girls tomorrow and we'll go over their schedule and changing times, etcetera, etcetera. Do you even know etcetera? Listen to me! Ha!" My mother turned to me.

"Dicky, am I forgetting anything for Olive, sweetie?"

I shrugged and tried to focus on my game, but I was enthralled by Olive's silence, which was obviously unnerving my mother.

"Oh! Yes, I left a box of hand-me-downs under your bed. Some old things of Ginger's, and some of Dicky's, which should fit you. He's grown out of a lot of things lately. Ha!"

Then she was gone and I was alone with this new, silent person.

Olive looked around for a moment, sighed deeply, and sat down next to me on the couch. She laid back and rubbed her eyes with the meaty parts of her palms, which made her arm muscles look even bigger than they had before. Her legs were spread wide, like a boy would sit, and she seemed loose and limber where she had seemed taut and rigid just moments before.

She looked at the television and then at me. "What are you playing?"

"*Final Fantasy 12*," I told her, knowing she wouldn't know what I was talking about.

"Really? The last one I played was ten. Well, ten-two, actually. Which was weird, wasn't it? Why wasn't that eleven?"

"You play video games? How?" I didn't mean to say *how*, it just came out.

"You mean, how could a poor maid afford to play a video game? Well, I wasn't rich growing up, but I had four brothers and sisters, and a Playstation was a pretty good way to get one present that would make all five of us happy. And my dad knew a lot of rich people from the hotel he worked at so, now that I think about it, he probably got it secondhand."

"That is so cool. Do you want to take a turn?" I didn't have any friends that played video games.

"I've got to do some sewing. So how about I sit here while I sew and watch you play. Then we can both decide what you're going to do. That way it's like we're both playing."

This was awesome. I hadn't had anybody to play video games with in years. My dad had played with me back when I first started, racing against me in *Mario Kart* and stealing the controller from me to "show me" how to beat the bosses in *Chrono Cross*. But, especially after we moved to Hong Kong, he had less and less time to play video games with me. He was always at the office, and when he wasn't, he was sitting in his chair, drinking wine and playing on his laptop.

"But, I'm going to need a favor, Dick. You're going to have to show me the places your mom will look to see if I've cleaned."

227

⇒ 2 ⇐
Olive masters the mundane

Olive quickly became a part of our daily lives. She took to her daily tasks quickly, and by her third day was accomplishing everything Ginger had and more. After a week, her routine ran like clockwork. It would change slightly when school began again. I'd have to get to The American School in Happy Valley by eight and my sister Essie would have to get to nursery school by nine. Then she'd only have Sophie, my eight-month-old sister, to look after during the day. The streets of Central Hong Kong would also be busier. Many of the really rich people, the people who lived at the very top of Victoria Peak, left Hong Kong for July and August because it was too hot. They would go to France, or London, or visit family. These were the same folks who spent December in Switzerland, or Norway. These were the people my parents aspired to be.

Olive's current schedule, however, involved a lot of me. Ginger had pretended to like my company but I could tell she was happier when I wasn't around. I'd sometimes come home from school and find her doing dishes or making dinner with her headphones on, dancing around the kitchen. She'd have her eyes closed and she'd move so freely, like a piece of pasta rolling around in the butter on the bottom of a dish. Then I'd say hi and she'd straighten up, take her headphones off, and put something that I liked on the radio. I'd tell her to listen to her music, that I didn't care what she played, and she'd say, "Oh I like this a lot. It's hip. This is what the kids are talking about in school, right?"

If Olive changed around me, however, it was for the better. When my mother was around, which was often, Olive would move through the apartment as silent as a cat. When it was just her and me, though, she was different. She'd pretend to struggle with her chores, lugging the vacuum cleaner around like it was a bag of rocks and wiping fake sweat from her forehead. She would watch me play video games and quiz me about what was happening. Once, early on in her time with us, she was in another room and yelled, "Are they talking? Tell me what they are saying!" I read the lines of dialogue to her. I was nervous. I was a good reader, really good for my age, but reading out-loud made me embarrassed.

"You're reading like a list of ingredients. Read the characters. I am here cleaning up your dirt, the least you can do is entertain me!"

My cheeks were bright red, but we were alone in the apartment. I spoke in the most raspy, evil voice I could come up with: "Give me the crystal! I will seal you away in the dark realms for eternity!"

"Oh is that the bad guy? Very scary," Olive said as she dusted knick knacks and picture frames.

"I command you to stop. I am the queen of this land," I continued, now in my best princess voice.

"Oh she sounds tough. Like me!"

From then on, I would narrate my video games to Olive when we were alone together. I found myself choosing to play games with more dialogue so that I could perform for her. She would always ask me questions about the characters, the worlds the games took place in, the items I would use.

Olive would wake up every morning at 5:30 and prepare breakfast for everyone. One morning I got up to go to the bathroom and saw her in the kitchen, a towel on her head, mixing eggs in a bowl, setting bread on a plate in front of the toaster, stirring formula in bottles and shoving them in the refrigerator.

My dad woke up every morning at 6:30, his eyes puffy and red, and Olive would throw the eggs in the pan and toast the bread and have him fed and out the door. Olive would never linger while my parents ate. While my dad wolfed down breakfast with CNN International blaring on the television, she'd take Fledermaus for his first walk of the day. When she returned, she'd wake Essie and Sophie and feed them. Essie always demanded that her orange juice be served in a champagne glass, and Olive would refer to her as "your highness" and then would read to her while she balanced Sophie on her hip.

After the girls ate, Olive would pick an activity for the girls—which usually meant keeping the baby on her hip and finding something for Essie to color—while she mixed a smoothie for my mother. She wouldn't dare wake my mother directly, but the blender was loud enough to do the job. My mother would shuffle in, grab her smoothie and then shut herself in her office to "check emails" for a couple of hours, which I knew from spying meant either napping on the day-bed or buying shoes on the internet.

When I'd wake up, Olive would make a show of how late it was, and then have me assist her in making whatever I wanted for breakfast. I think if I'd thrown a tantrum she would have immediately just made it for me by herself, but I liked being near her and I liked learning to do things in the kitchen. My parents had cooked when we'd lived back in Boston and I had always loved watching my dad cut meat and make sauces and my mom chop vegetables and mix salads. They hadn't cooked since we'd moved to Hong Kong.

Then, while I ate, Olive would either sew or, if my mother was walking around, clean things in the kitchen. Olive had a cycled cleaning schedule, making sure that every inch of the apartment was scrubbed at least once a week, but she would always do the kitchen, my parents' bathroom, and all of the mirrors if she had free time because those were the places my mother would notice first.

Eventually my mother would leave for an appointment, either coffee with a friend or a massage or a visit to Harbour City or Pacific Place, her favorite malls. Sometimes she would take Essie along with her in a stroller, leaving Olive with me and the baby. On rare occasions, my mother would stay at the apartment, sitting in her office and cutting inspiration pictures from magazine or talking on the phone with the accountant. I always felt weird with my mother around. If she saw me playing a video game she would tell me that I should be reading a book, which I preferred to do at night. Or she would ask me to help with her mood boards, or ask me about tennis lessons, or ask me if I had heard anything from my friends about what their parents were up to.

On these days, Olive would ask me if I wanted to run errands with her. We'd take the Central Escalator down to the wet market on Graham Street, where Olive would pick still-living seafood out of small aquariums in front of open-air shops. When the fishmonger wasn't looking she would tap the side of a container with her foot and wash the disturbed fish swim around. Then she'd choose the ones she wanted.

"How do you know which ones to pick?" I asked her once.

"You need to look in their eyes. If their eyes are clear, the fish is still alive, which means it will be freshest."

She went silent for a moment, like she was debating whether to keep talking. Then she turned to me and said,

"Plus, you should always look something in the eye before you hurt it."

⋙ 3 ⋘
In which the rules of Hong Kong Sundays are established and promptly broken

Sundays were Olive's day off. It was a rule in Hong Kong, that all of the maids got the entirety of Sunday off. My mother, for some reason, rebelled against this idea. I think she knew she shouldn't, but like picking a scab she couldn't help herself. She had argued with Ginger about it on more than one occasion. I had thought that she'd be better with Olive, particularly as Olive did twice as much work during the week as Ginger had ever done. At first, she had let Olive have her day. Olive would dress in her clothes from home, beautifully sewn tunics and light pants, grab her phone and her book bag and get on the escalator down the hill. I had seen what the maids did on Sunday. It was amazing. They covered every inch of public space in Hong Kong with sheets of cardboard and then sat on them. Some would fold the edges up, and the maids would be like butchers, bakers, and candlestick makers bobbing on the cement sea of Hong Kong. They'd gather in groups, some as small as three and some as large as thirty, and play cards, eat, nap, braid each others' hair, and all sorts of other things on their little cardboard picnic blankets. Olive told me that some girls got up as early as three in the morning in order to get the best space for their friends.

The Hong Kong government had a special rule that applied to the construction of buildings. Depending on the amount of space the building took up, the owners of the building had to offer a corresponding amount of "public space" as a form of payment to the city. So in addition to the sidewalks, bridges, parks, and walkways, you would find groups of maids on the roofs of skyscrapers, in the lobbies of malls, even on the little platforms between sections of the Central escalator.

They did this in every inch of Hong Kong, from Hong Kong Island to Kowloon to Lantau to Lamma. Apparently they even did it in the New Territories, a massive spread of land on the mainland side of Hong Kong beyond Kowloon and, according to my mother, beyond civilization.

Eventually Olive made friends with other maids, particularly with a few Vietnamese girls, most of whom worked further down the island from us. Her closest friend, Diamond, the only one who also worked on Conduit Road, would often walk back with her late on Sundays. I would watch out the window for Olive, eager to catch a glimpse of her under the streetlights. She and Diamond would walk up the hill, cheeks red from the sun ("and cheap beer" my mother said once), arm in arm, swaying and smiling. I was so jealous.

After a time my mother began to infiltrate Olive's Sundays. At first it was requests for little favors, asked in baby voice late on Saturday night. "Olive, sweetie, would you drop this package off at the Chesterton's on Hollywood Road on your way to play with your friends?" was the first request.

Eventually she dropped some of the sweetness. "Olive, since Barney's out of town on business and I'll be watching all three kids tomorrow *by myself*, can you pick up these groceries on your way back home tomorrow?" She handed Olive a list.

Olive didn't complain, but we all knew that Olive had shopped ahead on Saturdays so that we would be set for Sunday, and that she didn't come back until around nine, hours after the grocery store closed on Sundays. I waited all day to see if Olive would finally rebel, stand up to my mother. Still, I was happy when she appeared at six on the nose with a few bags of groceries. She had chosen us.

Olive came into the apartment, blank-faced, and emptied the bags of groceries. She kept her shoes on, which I had never seen her do. My mother appeared and said, "Olive, thank goodness you're home. Can you please take those filthy shoes off? Essie wants me to play Barbies with her but Sophie's giving me so much trouble. Can you take them off of my hands for a little while? I have to get some work done. Today has been a complete write-off."

Olive never changed her expression. It was obvious that

she had been planning on unpacking the groceries and heading back out. She went to the door, took off her shoes, neatly stacked them in their drawer, and returned to the kitchen. She took Sophie from my mother and continued to unpack groceries while balancing the baby on her hip.

Several weeks later, Olive was folding laundry on the couch next to me while I played a videogame. Olive was asking me about Ivalice, which was the world where *Final Fantasy 12* was set. My mother padded into the living room, her robe wafting around her in the air conditioning like a royal vestment. "Olive, I'll need you to take Dicky to his tennis match tomorrow morning before you go out and play."

Olive stiffened momentarily, then nodded and grabbed a pair of my mother's underwear from the ironing board, folded it into a tiny square, and placed it into the basket with the rest.

"Is that okay with you?" my mother asked, though I am sure she'd seen Olive nod.

"Yes, Mrs. Bumble," Olive said.

"Okay great. Barney and I have brunch with the Corneys tomorrow and their nanny is going to watch Essie and Sophie. They have a maid *and* a nanny! Can you imagine the luxury? I would get so much more done. Dicky needs to be at his match at ten. You can just drop him off and Barney will come and get him after brunch."

The next morning Olive had me up and dressed for my match by nine. She made me breakfast and then grabbed my tennis bag and marched me out the door. We walked up Conduit Road to Old Peak Road. Old Peak Road was insanely steep, and I got winded just walking up the small part of the road where Conduit met Old Peak and the LRC. The LRC was the Ladies Recreation Club, which was not just for ladies, despite its name, and according to my mother was the "most prestigious athletic club in Hong Kong." I was a part of a tennis club there, and even though I sucked, my mother decided that it was a good networking opportunity for her and my dad to meet other parents of kids my age. However, they had never been to a match.

"Olive, will you stay and watch me play?" I asked. I didn't want her to go and play with Diamond. I didn't want her to like Diamond better than me.

Olive smiled and said, "Of course I can."

She followed me inside. A woman at the front desk caught up to us and whispered to Olive, "Miss, I'm afraid your attire does not meet the dress code. If you'd like, you can purchase something from the pro shop."

This kind of phrase would have horrified my mother. I had seen it before, like when we'd arrived at a restaurant that required a reservation and did not have one. Olive just laughed.

"Can you tell me what part of my outfit is breaking the rules?"

The woman looked at Olive, in her peach tunic, calf-length pants, and sandals, as if she were insane.

"I am afraid that shorts and t shirts are only permitted for those participating in sporting activities, and closed-toe shoes are a requirement for everyone, outside of the showers.

"It's okay, Olive, you don't have to watch me," I told her.

Olive looked around, surely seeing all of the lighter skinned members breaking the rules.

She turned to me and said, "I'll be right outside. I'll meet you afterwards."

"But don't you want to go meet your friends?" I asked.

"I want you to go and have fun and I'll be here when you're finished."

She turned to the attendant. "Is it okay if I wait outside for him?"

I was down 3-0 by the time I heard her. Olive was standing on the top floor of the parking garage attached to the LRC, wedged in between a Jaguar and an Escalade, waving and cheering. "Hit to his right side! It goes into the net!" she yelled.

She must have meant his backhand. I wasn't good enough to execute this plan very well, but I lost more respectably than usual, 6-4, 6-4. I hit all of my serves to his backhand, which was in fact pretty bad. I found myself playing much better with Olive watching, running for balls I usually just let land. Olive cheered loudly, her accented English echoing through the court, and the parents of my opponent watched her from their seats with their mouths hanging open.

Afterwards, Olive walked me back home.

"You are very talented," she said to me as we walked.

"I haven't won a match yet."

"You were close. If you keep exercising, you'll get those extra balls and win. It's like a video game. You use strategy and beat your opponent. You're a natural." She seemed exhilarated by the experience.

We got home around one in the afternoon. Olive didn't leave to meet her friends. Instead, she sat next to me and sewed while I played video games. When my parents returned home, my dad swayed back and forth as he told me how the measure of a brunch spot was the quality of their Bloody Marys, and that I should never forget that.

Olive walked into the kitchen and I heard her greet my mother. My mother spoke to her in one of her loud whispers, "Olive, we received a call from the McCallisters. Dicky played their son in his match this morning. They said that you were acting in an entirely inappropriate fashion today. I am so embarrassed. I am shocked by your behavior."

I was angry for Olive. I wanted to go and confront my

mother. But I just sat there, raging. I expected Olive, as always, to give into my mother. To apologize. But this time she did not. I gasped when she said, "Today was my day off. I was not working for you there. So how I acted in my free time was not your concern."

My mother didn't speak for a moment, and I guessed that her face had gone red as it did when she was angry or embarrassed.

"Olive, you were representing this family in a negative way. You were setting a bad example for Dicky. That is unacceptable."

"Mrs. Bumble, do you know what a bad example would be? Breaking the law. And by asking me to work on Sunday that is what you are doing."

Even my father had perked up. He sat up in his chair, and looked towards the kitchen. I had expected him to rush to my mother's defense, or at least look angry. Instead, he looked scared, like he was wondering if he could sneak away without being noticed.

"What is it that you want from me?" My mother's voice was more of a yell now. "I feed you, I clothe you, I put a roof over your head. What do you want from me?"

From her volume and gasps for breath, it was evident that my mother was in full performance mode. I was sure she had her arm to her chest, grasping her heart as she did when she was at her most dramatic. It was also clear from her tone that her question was rhetorical, but Olive still chose to answer her.

"What do I want from you? More, ma'am. More time. The time I am owed."

I could tell this hit a nerve. "More time. You want more time? In addition to free room and board, free clothes, and a salary? And you're asking for more time?"

Olive's voice was an ocean of calm in contrast to my mother's gasps and wails.

"Yes. Please, ma'am, I want some more."

4

An important segment on handbags,
details of which the canny reader will remember

After that there was a throat-tightening amount of tension in the room whenever my mother and Olive were both in it. Olive was given her Sundays off, but my mother made sure to complain about "the lazy maid" in every conversation on the phone. Olive acted as she always had, curious and inquisitive with me, Essie, and Sophie, and with a face of stone around my mother. One morning, my mother's friend Patrice came to our apartment for coffee. Olive laid out a spread of coffee, tea, and pastries, and then disappeared into her room to do laundry. Olive asked me to play with Essie and Sophie in their room. If my mom had asked me I would have thrown a fit.

I could hear mom and Patrice in the kitchen, gossiping about their friends, complaining about how hot Hong Kong was in the summer and about all of the Asians in Central who had no sense of personal space. I asked Essie what she wanted to play with and she said "Barbies!"

I preferred Barbies to trucks but I had outgrown both by that point. Still, I pulled Essie's box of Barbies from the shelf. I set Sophie on my lap, where she belched and cooed, and began to take the Barbies out, one by one.

As we played, I heard Olive enter the kitchen and offer more coffee to Patrice and my mother.

"Patrice, I didn't even tell you that Olive is from Vietnam. Weren't you just there?"

"Yes, it was divine!" Patrice replied. Patrice always spoke to everyone as if she were speaking to them from across a crowded room.

"You know, what always strikes me about Vietnam is how French it is," Patrice continued. "It's like a little French oasis in Southeast Asia. So lovely and colonial. Don't you think, Olive?"

I didn't hear Olive say anything, but my mother said, "Patrice, I don't think Olive is from *that part* of Vietnam."

They both laughed.

Then, and I had to ask her later what she had said, Olive said, "*Oui il y a encore une grande influence française au Viêt-nam. Pour de bon ou de mauvais.*"

This time my mother said nothing but, Patrice, delighted, exclaimed, "Olive! *Vous parlez français?*"

"*Oui, madam.* More coffee?" From Olive's tone, I could tell that French lessons were over.

I continued to play with the girls but kept an ear to the door. After more gossip, Patrice said to my mother, "Oh Stephanie! I almost forgot to tell you. I was talking to Arthur about your hobby and he said that his colleague Rose is creating a new handbag line, and she wants it to represent flavors from the various parts of Hong Kong. It would be for next year's summer collection. And she doesn't have anyone from our circle, if you will, so your chances will be that much better. Rose will be looking at portfolios next month. Just call this number and tell them Arthur referred you. That will get you an appointment, no questions asked." I heard clinking and crunching as she searched around her handbag.

"Here's Rose's card."

My mother must have been genuinely excited because she didn't use the shrill fake-happy voice that she used when my sister showed her something she finger painted or my dad told her about a new account his agency had won. Instead, she sounded like a little girl, whispery and breathless. "Oh my goodness, Patrice. This means the world to me. Really. The world. I'll call her tomorrow."

It was moments like this that I wished I knew my mother

better. I knew that she hadn't been born rich, though she'd taken to it naturally. I knew that it had been her dream since she was a little girl was to be a designer. I knew that she had gone to school for design in New York and that she'd worked briefly as an art director at an advertising agency, where she'd met my father and they'd fallen in love and he had swept her off her feet. They had married quickly and nine months later, I was born. Since then, she had been working from home on her business, drawing and sewing and collecting. When I was really little, I remember her doing it all the time. But in Hong Kong, where she had more time, she did less.

"Well, it's just a referral, doll. And Lord knows you'll get no credit for it. But it's a foot in the door. Now, did you hear about the Wongs? Remember the wife, Kitty, the very articulate Chinese lady? Yes, they were at the Schmidt's Memorial Day party. Yes, the one with the boxed wine. My God, did Lara really think we wouldn't notice if she put it in a punch bowl with some fruit slices? Well, the Wongs got their daughter a Hong Kong passport through a loophole, but Kitty only has a Chinese passport, and now . . ."

They continued to chat. Olive came in to check on us, balancing a basket of laundry on her hip and smiling. Essie and Sophie had both fallen asleep, Sophie in her crib and Essie in a pile on the floor. I was pretending the Barbies were warriors waging battle against an invading troll brigade. I asked

Olive, "Would you ever think about making purses? You sew all the time. It sounds like that lady Patrice knows wants designers from every part of Hong Kong. You should go!"

To my surprise, Olive laughed.

"Can you see me showing up there at the same time as your mother? She would kill me. Or fire me. Probably kill me, because then I'd be fired too." I just stared at her, I'd never heard her say anything about my mother before. She usually avoided the subject.

I expected her to say, "let's just keep this between us," like Ginger would say when she said something bad about my parents. Instead, Olive straightened up and said, "I forgot myself for a moment. It's not my place to speak to you about your parents. My apologies."

"It's okay, Olive," I said.

"No it's not Dicky. That is not how this world works. You need to learn that."

⋙ 5 ⋘
Olive, being goaded by Mrs. Bumble, makes a choice

After the Sunday disaster, I think that we were all waiting for my mother to snap again. So when she came home in a rage one Thursday night, it was almost a relief. I saw so much anger on her face as she came through the door that I thought Olive had done something truly terrible, impossible as it seemed.

"Olive? Olive, where the *hell* are you?"

Olive came out from the kitchen, actually looking surprised.

"Olive. Ashley McCallister told me that she has seen you just *leave* a puddle of Fledermaus's pee on the sidewalk right in front of their building."

"That's not true," Olive said.

"So now you're calling my friend a liar?"

Olive kept her stance firm, but kept her eyes to the floor. I decided to try for distraction.

"Mom, Olive always uses the water bottle after Fledermaus pees. I go with her sometimes."

My mother turned to me and got the look on her face that she used at school meetings, the fake smile and the squinted eyes. "Darling, she does it when you're there because that's how people act in front of the people they work for."

I would be lying if I said that my ten year old self didn't feel a surge of power being called someone's boss, but I saw Olive swallow hard as my mother said it. At the time I thought it was her pride. But I now feel like it was watching her hard work being stripped away. Olive had been raising me in the months she had been with us, and she was watching her work be undone.

"Olive, I'm sure your mother raised you in disgusting conditions and you don't know any better, but this is too much."

I figured that Olive would just let my mother rant for a while, but she spoke back.

"Don't talk about my mother."

I don't know if it is a trick of memory, but I think my mother smiled, triumphant in finally finding something that could rattle Olive.

"Why? Why shouldn't I? What kind of woman raises an entitled brat who doesn't know how to clean up after herself?"

My mother was rambling, like she herself knew she was going too far but couldn't stop herself.

Olive raised her eyes from the floor and stared right into my mother's eyes. "Don't you dare talk about my mother."

As soon as the word 'mother' passed Olive's lips, my mother slapped her, hard across the mouth.

It was shocking and made little sense. Olive was angry, but hadn't been rude. I expected Olive to recoil. To put her hands up. To leave.

Instead, she slapped my mother back. It was quick and loud.

My mother's reaction was so overblown that I looked around to make sure that she hadn't fallen against something and been impaled. She screamed a blood-curling scream, right out of a horror movie, and then gasped, over and over, her lips puffing like one of the fish at the wet market.

She grabbed me and ran to the girls' room, shutting us in

247

with them. She pulled me close, hugging me like she hadn't done since I was little, and pulled her cell phone out.

She called the police. I couldn't believe my ears. We heard a rush of footsteps around the apartment and then the slamming of the front door. Then the apartment was silent until we heard sirens several minutes later.

⇒ 6 ⇐
Detailing Olive and Dick's correspondence

As it turns out, it was very easy to have a domestic worker's visa revoked, particularly one that was accused of a crime. Finding her, however, was a completely different matter. Olive had vanished. She took only her few meager belongings with her. I think my mother was disappointed that she hadn't stolen anything. She went through her jewelry five times just to be sure.

My mother was wrong, however. Olive had stolen something. A picture of me, Essie, and Sophie from the bookshelf in the living room. I noticed it was gone and my heart sang. I searched the house for a note, a secret message that she had left only for me, but found nothing.

Soon we had a new maid, Candy, who was from the Philippines and cost extra because no one else wanted to come live with us. Candy spoke mostly Spanish and loved to sneak me cookies when my mother wasn't looking. But I could not stop thinking about Olive. I knew she was in Hong Kong. I wrote her letters, telling her how Essie, Sophie, and I were doing, how we missed her, and how we were on her side in the whole slapping incident.

I decided to take action. I put the letters I had written to Olive in an envelope. I was about to seal it when inspiration struck, and I ran to my mother's office to retrieve one more item for the envelope. The card that my mother had received from Patrice, the one with the purse lady's number on it. I sealed it up and wrote "Olive" across the front. I volunteered to take Fledermaus for his walk while Candy made dinner. I walked him up Conduit Road, back and forth, until Diamond came out with her family's dog, a Shiba Inu named Puffin. She turned the other way when she saw me. I hustled to catch up with her, which was hard because both her and Puffin were in much better shape than Fledermaus and I.

Finally we caught them and Diamond said, "Please go away."

"No," I said. "I know Olive is still in Hong Kong. Can you give this to her?"

I handed her the envelope. She just looked at it. "Olive is back in Vietnam. I don't know her address."

"Please give this to her. It's from me. It's important."

Diamond stared at me for a long time. She was shorter

and wider than Olive, and wore much tighter clothing. Her face seemed to fall naturally into a suspicious expression. Finally, she said, "I'll throw this out for you." Then she took the envelope from me and walked away.

A week later I convinced a very stressed Candy to let me walk Fledermaus by myself again. My mother had been in a daze since Olive had left, alternating between frantic sessions in her office preparing for her big presentation at Patrice's husband's company and stretching out on the daybed with a big glass of red wine, staring out the window. When I asked her if it was okay if I walked Fledermaus by myself, she didn't answer, so I took it as a yes.

I waited outside of Diamond's house until her and Puffin arrived. She said nothing, but walked a long distance down Conduit Road until it turned back on itself and became the pedestrian-only Peak Trail. She and Puffin looked fresh as daisies, but Fledermaus and I were on the verge of death, panting and sweating.

"Olive sent this from Vietnam. Read it then give it back to me."
She handed over a letter.

Dear Dick,

I wrote you a whole letter saying that I was back in Vietnam. But I threw it away because I don't want to lie to you. I am still in Hong Kong, living deep in the city on Kowloon side.

You know how crowded we thought it was on Hong Kong Island? Well, Mong Kok, where I live now, makes the island seem abandoned by comparison! One of the other girls, Jackie, told me that there are 350,000 people per square mile in Mong Kok, the densest it is in the world. It pulses with people, making it seem even hotter than it already is. And the air is bad here. I wear a scarf over my mouth while I work, and when I go to bed at night it is black with soot.

You know, it reminds me very much of the Rabanastre city in your Final Fantasy game, full of high buildings and dark alleys, small shops and interesting characters. How is that going? Please write to tell me what has happened.

It's funny how you asked me once if I would make purses. Now I sew knock-off purses all day long. I work for a woman, Fa Gin, who runs many shops in the Ladies' Market on Tung Choi Street. She calls all of the girls who work for her, most of them former domestic helpers like myself, "her little urchins." She takes more than her share from the purses we sell, but no one here can sew like me so I am able to negotiate with her. You must make sure that you hone your talents: your imagination, your storytelling, your kind spirit and listening ear. Someday you may have to depend on them.

Though most of my days are spent sewing morning into night, on Sundays I get the day to myself. Just like I did when I worked for your mother. Ha ha ha.

I avoid the parts of the city near the MTR stations, because the police wait there and ask women like me for our papers. But I do explore. Most often, I walk through the Yuen Po Street Bird Market, where thousands upon thousands of beautiful birds sing to each other from the cages, strung together along the fronts of shops. They sit there and wait for tourists to come and buy them, to take them away to sit alone in their cold homes. But when I walk down the street, I don't think about that. I listen to them sing to each other, watch them groom their beautiful feathers.

Thank you for the gift in your note, but I do not know if I can use it. Not because it is a risk, which it is, but because your mother gave me much more than she took away. That said, if I have lost so much of my honor already, what would the consequences be of losing more? That is not a good message for me to be sending to you, but I do not want to tell you anything but the truth. I hope that someday we see each other again, but you must not ever come here. Still, if we keep this a secret, and know that I am wrong to ask you to keep a secret from your parents, we can keep annoying Diamond by passing notes through her.

Sincerely,

Olive, the Urchin

≥ 7 ≤
Wherein Olive Urchin and Stephanie Bumble
take divergent paths

A few days later, my mother came into the apartment looking sadder than I had ever seen her. When Candy saw her, she muttered something about having to fold laundry and disappeared into her room, Sophie on her hip. My father was working late and I was watching Essie color while I drew pictures of my favorite video game characters for a comic I was working on.

It was disturbing to see her look so sad. Though my mother was expressive, she rarely showed any real emotion. She walked to the fridge and pulled out a bottle of white wine from inside. It was three-fourths full and she poured its entirety into a big glass. Then she went into her office and shut the door.

I thought that maybe I should go comfort her, ask her what was wrong. But I didn't.

When my father came home he didn't even say hello. He went straight to my mother's office and shut the door.

Through the door, I heard her wail and scream and weep. Eventually, she managed to tell my father what had happened. She had gone to Patrice's husband's office and the woman who she had been supposed to show her purses to, Rose Nguyen, had declined to even look at her handbags.

She told my father how stupid she was, how she couldn't believe that she had let herself get her hopes up. Of course this was another disappointment, like everything else in her life, she said.

Months passed, and my mother sank into a deep depression. Then, one Sunday, I came out to the kitchen to find my mother clutching *The South China Morning Post*, her knuckles white. I had just settled into my seat at the breakfast table, waiting for Candy to give me something to eat, when my mother threw the paper down on the table and then picked up her coffee cup and hurled it at the wall. Her face was a mask of rage, but I was more used to her angry face than her sad one so it was slightly preferable.

She stalked out of the room and I grabbed the paper from the table. It was open to the *Style* section, and there, staring up at me from the page, was Olive. She was working hard at a sewing machine, a fresh tattoo of a songbird on a tree branch stretched across her bicep. Behind her stood a striking Asian woman in a red business suit, looking on with a smile. Above the picture was the title "Real Life Cinderella" and below was a story.

When I read it, I couldn't believe my eyes.

"It's just the best story," Nguyen said. "She just showed up out of the blue, with the most beautiful samples. I asked her where she was from, and she said that she knew I was looking to capture all of Hong Kong with my new collection, so why not show the maids? Can you believe it? We all have one or two in our homes but it never even crossed my mind. Brilliant, isn't it?"

Nguyen adjusts her pearl necklace before continuing. "I wanted to hire her on the spot. But then came the question of her visa. You see, her last job had gone south fast, she worked for some demon, we all know how it goes. And—this is what is going to make the headlines—we discovered that she is my niece! Can you believe it? We just took a few visits down to the immigration building, and I called my good friend Jiang Shan, who works on the Legislative Council, and her paperwork was all sorted out!"

And finally

The fortunes of those who have figured in this tale are nearly closed. What little remains for me, their historian, to relate can be told in few a simple words.

It has been nine years. Olive, as I am sure you know, is the owner and chief designer of one of Asia's most famous fashion companies, Olive Urchin. Her company is known for its fair pay and hours, and particularly for its ban on any Sunday work communication.

Olive and I have remained great friends over the years and she told me the real story of how she got her lucky break. Rose Nguyen, born Nguyen Chi Long, was not really Olive's aunt, of course. But when a dirty, underfed Olive came into Rose's company's head office, the girl at the desk asking where her "mistress" was, Rose by some twist of fate had left her office door ajar and had heard the Vietnamese accent in her response (which had been, "where's yours?").

Rose took one look at the purses Olive had brought along and offered her a job on the spot. Olive, to her credit, then burst forth with the story of her situation, that her and her siblings had been orphaned and she'd come to Hong Kong as a maid but had committed a terrible crime. Rose, who had wanted to slap more than one Mid-Levels Hong Konger, asked about Olive's mother.

"She was quiet. She loved for us all to take a bus down to the markets floating in the Mekong, where she'd grown up, and we'd drink water with sugar cane and peanuts and ride bicycles around the dirt roads. She cooked *pho bo* at least three times a week. She loved the noise of Saigon. She always told us that we could have the entire world if we worked hard. She worked every day of her life, and she taught all five us a skill that we would be able to use to feed ourselves."

At this, Rose smiled, and said, "Olive, it is obvious to me from what you say that your mother and I were *sisters.* Both from Vietnam. Which makes you my niece. Which means it is my duty to have you with me in Hong Kong as family."

This sounds rare, but when anyone has a lot of money anywhere, and Rose Nguyen had a lot of money even by Hong Kong standards, it is pretty easy to convince the government to give you what you want, particularly Hong Kong's government. Soon, Olive had her own apartment in Wan Chi and soon after that her brother and sisters had come to live with her. After a few short years, Rose invested in Olive's own venture, Olive Urchin, and the world knows them as one of Hong Kong fashion's first families.

This is Olive's story, not my family's, but I will say that my mother and father both stayed true to character. After reading about Olive, my mother did all that she could to have her arrested, fired, deported, and shamed. My father stayed out of her way, glass of wine in one hand and laptop in the other. After a while, when it became clear that Rose Nguyen's money and word went further than my mother's money and word, my mother gave up, but gossiped horribly about them for some time until she found herself invited to less and less functions.

My mother went the way of her friends after that, choosing her opinions strategically and spending her days attending brunches and charity events, though she was more busy with childcare and housework than most of her peers.

You see, though the labor may be cheap, the maids of Hong Kong are close knit and loyal, and my mother was never able to find another one once Candy quit following a wild goose chase of Sunday errands.

I don't know my mother well. I never have. She is utterly foreign to me. But she is not foreign to Hong Kong. She is a part of the world at the tippity-top of Hong Kong Island, above the treeline of wealth that prevents the common folk from setting down roots in its soil. Where all homes, large and small, are cages. Cages for the most beautiful birds you will ever see, locked away with no one but each other to listen to their songs.

ACKNOWLEDGEMENTS

So many people helped tangentially, directly, and inspirationally to make this book happen. First and foremost, I want to thank my friend, Louis Flint Ceci, who is not only the editor and publisher of this collection but who has served as a mentor to me and a gold miner for the stories themselves. I am so thankful for your support, guidance, and brilliance.

While researching, I found several books vital to my understanding of specific times and places. These are Marc McCutcheon's *The Writer's Guide to Everyday Life from Prohibition through World War II* (Writer's Digest Books), Ruth Goodman's *How to be a Victorian: A Dawn-to-Dusk Guide to Victorian Life* (Liveright Publishing Company), and F.W. Evans' *Shaker's Compendium*. I also relied heavily on Suni Williams and Karen Nyberg's videos from the International Space Station and on information found in The National Archives of the UK (TNA).

I would love to thank each of my closest friends by name, but I'm terrified of leaving someone out. Lovers, you know who you are and I adore you. I do have to individually thank

Graham Warsop and Debbie Hichens for their time, support, and encouragement, and Kim Smith, Nikki Kurt, and Nichole Rousseau-McAllister for reading and offering your trusted reactions over the years.

I owe a great deal my teachers, friends, and colleagues at Georgia College for being the first readers of many of these pieces. Your feedback was incredibly helpful and your energy so inspiring. Thank you to John Sirmans, Aubrey Hirsch, Cecilia Woloch, Marty Lammon, Laura Caron, Melinda Martin, Bruce Gentry, Georgia Knapp, Julia Wagner, Demi Doyle, Shane Moritz, Jim Owens, Ian Sargent, Shannon Skelton, Monic Ductan, Ruby Holsenbeck, Penny Dearmin, Laura Martin, Adam Nannini, Kera Yonker, Abbie Lahmers, Ernie Montoya, Roe Sellers, Noah Devros, Marshall Newman, Kristie Johnson, Ryan Loveeachother, Jennifer Watkins, Dani DiCenzo, Tara Mettler, and Isabel Avecedo. And thank you most of all to Peter Selgin, whose insightful, thorough feedback helped shape most of these stories.

I want to bring attention to the two writers who had the biggest impact on the writing of this book. The first is, appropriately, my very first creative writing professor: Kerry Neville. Thank you for inspiring me with your writer's brain and your warrior's heart. And to Allen Gee: thank you for your critical eye, your breadth of knowledge, and the generosity with which you share it.

I'm so lucky to have a big family in South Africa and in the United States, and I want to thank all of you for your love and support. Specifically, I want to thank the McClelland/ Huff/Williamson/Griffin families, particularly Justin Williamson, Julie Williamson, Kimberley Clow, James Clow, Marlene Griffin, Kathy Newtzie, Kay Beck, and Pam Freeman.

Thank you to Casey McClelland for being my best friend and most trusted collaborator. And to Virginia McClelland and Brian McClelland, thank you for loving me and believing in me. I adore you.

Finally, thank you to my beautiful husband, Simon Williamson. I love you.

About the Author

Before becoming a writer, Mike McClelland worked as a gravedigger, wedding singer, antique salesman, and as a marketing strategy director for clients like Toyota, MillerCoors, and Buffalo Wild Wings. Like Sharon Stone and the zipper, he hails from Meadville, Pennsylvania. He has lived on five different continents but now resides in Georgia with his husband and a menagerie of rescue dogs. His work has appeared in a variety of anthologies and literary journals and he frequently collaborates with his brother Casey, an abstract artist. He is a former member of WPP's prestigious marketing fellowship program and holds a B.A. from Allegheny College, a M.Sc. from The London School of Economics, and an M.F.A. in Creative Writing (Fiction) from Georgia College & State University. You can find him online at magicmikewrites.com. This is his first book.

CPSIA information can be obtained
at www.ICGtesting.com
Printed in the USA
FFOW02n0351140817
38729FF